THE ACCIDENTAL DAUGHTER

THE ACCIDENTAL DAUGHTER

LESLEY NELSON

Matador
9 Priory Business Park,
Wistow Road, Kibworth Beauchamp,
Leicestershire. LE8 0RX
Tel: (+44) 116 279 2299
Fax: (+44) 116 279 2277
Email: books@troubador.co.uk
Web: www.troubador.co.uk/matador

ISBN 978 1783061 334

British Library Cataloguing in Publication Data.
A catalogue record for this book is available from the British Library.

Typeset by Troubador Publishing Ltd, Leicester, UK

For 306 British and Empire soldiers
Shot at dawn by their own side
During the First World War
Officially pardoned 90 years later

And for Rifleman Maurice Foster
Who died in battle
No known grave

Contents

Prologue

Harry Hooker sat on a chair under the railway embankment. The blasting wind would have brought tears to his eyes if they hadn't been covered by a blindfold. As he was being strapped to the chair he asked not to be tied too tightly. No-one else spoke. Fifteen paces away a firing squad assembled; six kneeling, six standing. Their commanding officer mixed up the rifles and unloaded some of them so no-one would know whose bullet would be the killer. Harry was aware of a disc being pinned over his heart – the target. The officer called, "Fire!" Harry's head fell back, and the chair creaked with stress before toppling sideways. The firing squad turned and marched away while a doctor stepped forward to check that Harry was dead. The body was wrapped in a blanket and tipped into an anonymous grave.

PART ONE

CHAPTER ONE

Spring 1910

Harry sewed on the last button and stretched his long legs. The suit was finished. He glanced at his cousin, who usually made the deliveries. David was snoring with his shaggy head burrowed in tweed on the worktable. Harry chuckled; he'd walk to Savile Row himself and get a glimpse of the gorgeous hat maker David had been raving on about. He folded and wrapped the beautiful wool suit as he counted the chimes of St Anne's. It was eight o'clock – he'd been up all night. He peered at his tired face in the mirror and rubbed a chalk mark from his cheek. His dusty boots got a swift polish with a surplus shoulder pad before he hurtled down two flights of stairs and set off through the streets of Soho.

He was nineteen and felt taller than he was. A Savile Row tailor had taken Harry under his wing six months ago and was already giving him the measurements of important clients. The custom-made suit under his arm was for a Member of Parliament.

He chose a route through the street market, absorbing its ramshackle nature and pungent mix of émigré produce. Crossing the end of Poland Street, he sidestepped an unruly cricket match; neighbourhood boys, pushed out to play by mothers scrubbing floors, were using the traffic island as a wicket, and as Harry sidled past, the batsman hit the ball straight into the ladies' lavatory.

"Courage!" he yelled to the fielder, remembering the fierce attendant he'd faced in the days when he played. Was it Saturday already? He worked so hard the days merged. A whiff of coffee lured him into the French bakery, where he sat beside trays of cooling loaves. Calculating that the new suit would earn him at least three pounds, he ordered two soft buns with coffee. With his boot, he traced idle patterns in the sandy floor, knowing his father would think him reckless.

Ten minutes later he was standing in front of the Savile Row shop admiring the elegant lettering of Matthew Lock Bespoke Tailoring. A lean man in shirtsleeves appeared at the doorway.

"Good morning Mr Lock," said Harry, and his patron smiled.

"Harry, my boy, you've brought the suit yourself." He relieved Harry of his parcel and gave him a shrewd look.

"Come and meet my daughter Maudie. She's making hats for Black Ascot, but she'll have time for a cup of tea with you. She thinks I'm hiding you from her."

Harry didn't hesitate. He followed Mr Lock along a dark panelled passage to a workroom. The small bright space resembled a festive carnival float, with every surface masked by flowers, ribbons and feathers. His eyes were already blurring when he noticed the garlanded queen. Maudie appeared to be sitting on a bank of daisies, attaching black silk peonies to the crown of a straw hat. The final flower was held between strong teeth. She looked at her father, and when he introduced Harry, she carefully removed the blossom from her mouth before studying him with open curiosity. She wanted to know this master tailor her father was favouring like a son.

Harry stared back. David hadn't exaggerated: with her wide-boned face, speckled eyes and curvy mouth, she *was* gorgeous. He couldn't stand the idea that she might prefer his cousin, and a mad impulse sent him bounding into the room to fall on his knees at her feet, clowning devotion, claiming attention, making her laugh at his nonsense.

Maudie's father left the room shaking his head. He carried Harry's suit into the shop, wishing his wife was alive to enjoy the courtship of their only child.

Harry knew he should get back to Meard Street. He had another suit to work on, and David would be wondering ... He squashed a twinge of guilt by demanding to know why Maudie was working on a Saturday.

"Because the king has died," she said, and of course he knew. The race meeting at Ascot was three weeks' away and this year's visitors were expected to wear black. Gentlemen would be dressed in his fine broadcloth suits and ladies would be parading in Maudie's hats. The potential for a working partnership excited him, but Harry's attention was currently focused elsewhere. He was lost in the vision of feral curls escaping unchecked from the bun at the back of Maudie's head. As she cleared space for a tea tray, he absorbed the intimacy of a hairpin sliding from the bun to free another bouncy curl, and when she looked up to meet his gaze with her cool grey eyes, he was swamped with certainty. *This vital woman would be his wife.*

"Papa!" Harry burst through the door to find his father waiting for him at Meard Street, pacing over creaky floorboards while David tried to engage him with their plans for a shop. From the flare of his father's nostrils, it was evident he didn't want to listen to this rumpled nephew with impertinent ideas.

He smiled at his father, so impeccably groomed he could be on the way to a king's funeral. He touched the back of his neck under his father's gaze, fixed as it was on the thick black hair flopping over Harry's collar.

"You're working today?" There was reproach in his father's face, and Harry felt slugged by the weight of the Sabbath.

"I have to, Papa. I have to finish the Ascot orders." He saw the hurt in his father's eyes and felt mean. He'd learned everything he knew about tailoring from his father, and now he was working for another man who was not only well-established, but who had the most desirable daughter in the world. Harry was appalled with himself.

"Papa," he said, "Mr Lock often compliments you for all the skills you passed on to me." Including the work hours, he thought, and a childhood memory tugged Harry back under the table where he'd slept on a mattress with a tangle of cousins while his father tailored through the night. He looked at this admirable man preparing to leave and wanted to hug him. Instead, he offered his father a cigar Mr Lock had given him.

His father pocketed it with a grunt of thanks. "Remember your mother likes you to share the shabbos meal with us," he said in parting. Harry heard himself promising to be there next Saturday.

He waited until he heard his father's cautious tread on the stairs before collapsing into a lumpy armchair. "Why do I always disappoint him?"

"Because you're not his slave anymore," said David. "And don't start protesting."

"You, too," said Harry.

"Yes, and that's why I know what I'm talking about. He's jealous of Mr Lock."

"Come on, we've got work to do." Harry tried to lever himself out of the exhausted depths of the chair, but David pinned him down.

"One question," he said. "Did you meet Mr Lock's daughter this morning?"

Harry's face turned a hectic red. " She's a splendid hat maker, isn't she?"

"It's okay," said David. "No contest. She's too bold for me. But isn't she a *beauty*."

Through the summer, Harry wove her into his life. Both had absurdly long work days making fashionable clothes for the society events of the season, but Harry made time to nip out to the French bakery for butter croissants to share with Maudie during an early break. And if he heard the fruit cart clop by at midday, he ran to the market to buy her a punnet of raspberries picked that morning in Kent. He'd lived in Soho all his life and he knew how to give flavour to a life crammed with deadlines. His neighbourhood was a mix of emigrant French, Italian and Yiddish-speaking shopkeepers, and he was familiar with a number of food traders in Berwick Street. On Sunday, when he walked Maudie to Regent's Park, he carried a picnic of baguettes, chopped herring and small pickled cucumbers.

One weekend he persuaded his Uncle Aaron, who had a delivery business, to lend him a pony and trap for Sunday morning. He asked Maudie to wear her best hat and drive with him through Hyde Park.

"Only the privileged do that," she said, but he swayed her by modelling his borrowed top hat and provoking a sense of drama. By the time he drew up in Savile Row to collect her, Maudie had eased herself into a corseted dress that accentuated her nineteen-inch waist. She piled her hair high and pinned on a saucy feathered hat.

On the way back to the stables he confessed to her that it seemed stiff and unnatural parading in public.

"I felt like a poser," said Harry.

"I felt like one, too," said Maudie.

And that was it: he knew he loved her.

The next weekend they took a horsedrawn bus to Lyons Corner House and drank tea, watching a crowd gather outside. When they emerged, a full-scale demonstration had been mobilised by suffragettes. They lingered under the Votes for Women banners, and with Maudie's arm linked through his, he joined a spirited chorus of male bystanders in support of the movement. It seemed quite natural to him, in this land of opportunity his parents had brought him to.

The moment of solidarity clinched Maudie's resolve to accept Harry's proposal when it came. She already regarded him as an exotic catch; he was the son of Polish immigrants, and his foreignness intrigued her. She liked the aristocratic nose that dominated his bony face, and the watchful nightblue eyes shadowed by ferocious brows. And she knew her liberal father wouldn't object; he reserved all the best tailoring jobs for Harry.

She wasn't aware of his parents' opposition to the match until Harry's mother paid her a visit. Feeling scrutinised, Maudie glanced up from her work to see a tiny woman offering her a gloved hand to shake.

"Mrs Samuel Hooker," she announced. "Your father said I would find you here."

Maudie knew from Harry that his mother was a woman who expected to be obeyed; she hadn't met either parent before because Harry had wanted to 'prepare' them.

"I have come to ask you to release my son from his obligations to you," said Mrs Hooker, emphasising each word. Maudie looked closely at Harry's mother and saw a face shaped by suffering.

"I assure you…" she began, before the warning touch of gloved power silenced her.

"Forgive me," said Harry's mother, releasing her pressure on Maudie's arm, "but I *have* to speak. I have to tell you why I'm asking you this favour."

Maudie swept aside a heap of fabrics from a brocade-upholstered bench and offered her visitor a seat, hypnotised by this woman who was still trying to control Harry at the age of nearly twenty. His mother sat on the edge of the bench, observing the young woman who'd confused her son.

"Harry was three months old when we left Russia," she said. "We lost everything, but we had our son. If I'd been able to have more children, maybe I would be less – protective. But there were difficulties and Harry's arrival was a miracle." Her bead-bright eyes were unblinking.

"I thought you were Polish."

Harry's mother jumped to her feet. "We were Polish Jews living in the Russian Empire; swallowed up by a country whose emperors had always kept us outside its borders. Ha! By the time we left in 1891, Russia was the centre of the Jewish world. Such an *irony.*"

"Did you have to leave?"

Harry's mother sat down again and shut her eyes. "You clearly have no idea, do you? The Czar was assassinated. Life was intolerable after that." Her face was ice-white.

Maudie poured a tumbler of water from the jug on her worktable and watched Harry's mother drain the glass.

"Thank you," she said, accepting a refill, and as Maudie threaded a needle, she moved to stand. "I'm talking too much – and taking up your time." Maudie was about to protest, but she sensed an emotional trap.

"It's rude of me to work while you're here," she said, "but I promised my father I'd finish this hat today."

Harry's mother watched her sew a cascade of silk roses she'd made to the crown of a wide straw hat already shivering with feathers. She leaned forward to inspect an ornamental pin beside the hat and saw that the flower-shaped head was made from delicately carved ivory.

"Must be for a special occasion."

" A royal garden party," said Maudie. "The clients choose all these trimmings." Her hand swept over soft piles of ostrich plumes and velvet ribbons, trying to assuage her prickly visitor.

"And that?" Harry's mother pointed to a stuffed songbird.

Maudie frowned. "The Queen doesn't approve of wild birds being killed for fashion. I tell clients the grebe is nearly extinct because of the demand for its plumage, but if a customer wants a dead humming bird mounted on her hat, that's what I do."

Harry's mother sighed. Of course her son was enchanted by this spirited young woman. So lovely, too. Maudie mistook the sigh for grebe-sympathy as she sprang to open the door for a girl who'd brought them a tray of refreshments. Harry's mother asked for the lavatory, and when she returned to the brocade bench she had two cups of tea and a biscuit while Maudie added bunches of lacquered cherries to the extravagant hat. She was longing to be alone, but Harry's mother was clearing her throat.

"I didn't expect you to be interested in our history," she said. "I merely wanted you to know how much we lost. We lost everything but our faith. We placed our faith in Harry, and we knew that someday he'd marry a Jewish girl and we'd be blessed with grandchildren who'd become the lawyers and administrators forbidden in Russia."

Maudie held the hat between rigid fingers and the lacquered cherries clicked against each other.

"We were wretched with fear. We all had neighbours whose homes had been looted or burned. We all knew women who'd been brutally attacked. Our boys had to serve in the Russian Army – *never* allowed to be officers, but always prepared to fight for the empire. How could we bring up our son in such a country?"

Maudie looked up. How dare this woman with a face clawed by sorrow attempt blackmail with her painful history. She was like a small wild bird fighting extinction.

"Will you tell me about the journey to London?" At least she would hear about Harry's arrival as a baby.

His mother looked mollified. "We shared the ship from Libau with *ponies*." Her laugh was harsh. "Five days it took. Aaron managed horses when we had a farm, so he earned his passage looking after the animals during the voyage. We slept on deck with them. We had greatcoats to the ankles to keep us warm, and straw pallets for beds, which the ponies ate."

Maudie thought of the ride to Hyde Park in Aaron's trap, aware that she was already storing memories of her life with Harry in case there were to be no more.

"When we reached Hay's Wharf ..."

The door flew open and Maudie's father stood there looking apologetic. Harry's mother scrambled to her feet.

"Dear lady, I'm sorry for the intrusion, but a client has come to collect her hat from my daughter." His face relaxed when Maudie held out a flamboyant creation swathed in tulle.

"Perfect," he beamed, and swept from the room bearing the hat like a trophy.

Harry's mother was still standing. She held out a hand to Maudie. "Thank you for listening to me. I think I've said enough."

"More than enough," said Maudie to herself.

Harry was incensed when she told him about his mother's tactics. He put his arms round her shivering body and promised no-one would keep them apart.

"You're my life," he said, and Maudie covered his rough face with kisses. During a night of jumbled dreams she'd panicked, believing Harry would give her up to placate his immovable mother. She looked at him now, certainty locked in his blueblack eyes; he was immovable, too.

The meeting between mother and son was indigestible. Harry's father stoically finished a plate of meatballs while they nibbled at each other's arguments, and before Harry's mother brought more food to the table, he retreated to his sewing machine nearby with pains in his chest.

"There is no need to explain everything," he said. "Our son is intelligent enough to know why he does not have our permission to marry a gentile."

Harry's mother was adamant. "He *has* to be reminded of his roots." She raised her voice to be heard above the clatter of crockery she was clearing from the table.

Harry's father belched. "Go ahead. Leave me in peace. I have a jacket to make."

She sat opposite Harry. "You were too young to know anything about our life in the Pale."

"Mama! You've told me so *many* times. You and Papa were extraordinary the way you kept reinventing yourselves. You adapted like chameleons. When you were allowed to live in the countryside, you had a farm and an inn. When you had to move into town, Papa learned tailoring."

Harry's mother got up from the table. He knew his simplistic version of events in Russia was about to be enlarged in wrenching detail, and he held her gently by the shoulders. He spoke softly.

"This is your history, Matka, not mine. My life began when you brought me to Britain and changed the family name. You brought me up to be English, and now I'm going to marry an Englishwoman."

Harry's mother screamed. "Speak to him, Samuel."

"I have already." Harry's father mumbled, pins jutting from his mouth. "He's forbidden from marrying a Protestant."

She launched herself at Harry, pounding his chest with small bruising fists. "How *dare* you defy us. After all the sacrifices…" A welter of tears and hiccups drowned the familiar words, and for the second time that day, Harry embraced a trembling woman. He held his mother, remembering her own comforting hugs when he was a boy. He felt absolutely wretched, and completely resolute.

Chapter Two

April 1912

Light was streaming through cracks in the shutters when Maudie opened her eyes. She was in Harry's bed, in a room with a high ceiling and whitewashed walls. An oval mirror hung above the mantelpiece, and a washstand stood beside the burnished coal range. She pressed into Harry's lean back as he muttered in his sleep. She sniffed his skin and thought of toast.

Sliding from the bed, she opened the shutters and sat on the window seat, looking at Harry in daylight. "My husband," she whispered.

They'd been married a week. The wedding itself was a strained event because his parents refused to come. Harry had prepared himself for this, but their insistence on a family boycott surprised even his father's older brother, Aaron.

"Listen to me," he said. "Harry's a wonderful boy. He's a credit to you. Remember what you told him on the ship from Russia? You had him wrapped inside your overcoat against the wind. You told him we were heading for a country where he'd be allowed to live the life he chose."

Harry's father looked into Aaron's warm brown eyes, seeing that his brother would support the wedding that dashed his hopes for Jewish grandchildren.

"You will betray me," was all he said.

At the engagement party arranged by Maudie's father, Aaron did what he'd always planned to do with their mother's gold wedding ring: he gave it to Harry for his bride.

It weighed heavy in the bridegroom's hand. "Surely this should be kept for David," said Harry.

"Your concern does you credit, dear boy, but David will have our father's ring when he gets married." Aaron patted his arm. "It's what they decided."

Maudie's father celebrated the marriage by acquiring the first floor of the Meard Street house and setting it up as a workshop for David and the newlyweds. The condition was that all three worked for him exclusively. The spacious room was the width of the dilapidated Georgian house, with three grimy sash windows facing the street and a partitioned annexe for David's bed. The annexe had been advertised as 'Part of a Room to Let.'

Maudie felt a small domestic thrill that the second floor rooms belonging to Harry's family could now be a real home, and the old workroom would be their living space; a place where she could hang the picture of her mother. Harry and David were already speculating on how long it would be before they could afford to take on the first-floor lease from Maudie's father. They were mentally filling the room with machinists and pressers, felling hands and buttonholers, and savouring names for their own business.

"Hooker and Hooker," said David.

"Sounds like a fishmonger."

"Meard Street Tailors and Fitters?"

Harry shook his head. "Too prosaic."

David pulled at the knots in his curly hair. His hazelnut eyes swivelled round the room before he came up with "Ace Tailoring." Harry grinned at once. "Snappy! I like it." And after a pause, "Where did that come from?" David held up the sleeve of a jacket from his workpile.

"An ace up one's sleeve?"

Harry clapped him on the back. "Cunning," he said. "Punning!"

When Maudie casually reminded them about the millinery element of the business, Harry looked serious.

"Maud Lock Hats are already famous," he said. "Would you like a shop to display them?"

"No," said Maudie. "I was teasing you. I'm lucky to have a husband who respects my work."

He kissed her smiling mouth and led her by the hand into the workroom to select her space. She chose the fireplace end, next to the window framed by a vine growing from pavement level. It was the only plant in the whole of Meard Street, and according to her father, a miracle of nature: it survived the abuse of full-bladdered drunks to fruit every summer in the south-facing windows of three tenements.

When she left the house, Maudie leaned over the flowerpot barrel and picked out Woodbine stubs. She patted the twisted vine trunk before hurrying off to Savile Row to clear the millinery workroom at her father's shop. In a few months' time she'd be leaning out of the Meard Street window to snip black grapes for breakfast.

June 1914

"Harry."

He heard Maudie gasp his name as the audience streamed past them out of the cinema.

"The waters," she said, and Harry caught her as she doubled over.

"Lean on me." He wiped away the laughter tear hovering on her cheekbone as she braced herself against him. Charlie Chaplin had been the comic relief in *Making a Living* after a newsreel dense with preparations for war.

"I'm having a baby!"

"Not in this fleapit, my darling. Hang on." Harry hoisted her into his arms and staggered from the cinema, with a commitment to protect his wife and nearly-born child at all costs. He resisted defining the meaning of 'all costs' to himself because it sounded so final.

After his son's home birth, he watched his mother's stern face glow as she touched the surprising jet of hair on her grandson's head. It was her first visit to their home since the marriage. She'd stayed away for two years, always 'too busy' to accompany her husband to Meard Street; never asking about Maudie when Harry came to see her.

Yet here she was, permitting herself to welcome this blameless child, with Harry at her side saying: "Would you like to hold him, Matka?"

"Let him sleep," she said.

Harry thought of his tough little mother giving birth to him in a hostile country; fleeing with him to an unknown land to protect his future. His collar scratched his throat as he reflected on his own son's arrival at the brink of a world war.

4th August 1914

The workroom was heaped with khaki fabric. Harry and David worked through the order for military greatcoats while Maudie made small hats decorated with long plumes of Mephisto feathers. Baby Harald, known from the start as their lucky mascot Ace, slept in a basket beside her, and pale-faced Annie counted coat buttons into groups. She was David's bright little sister of fifteen, who made all the buttonholes. And it was she who stitched the gold braid to the admiral's uniform Harry finished after three difficult fittings at

Savile Row with the expanding client. Harry had been exasperated by all the extra work, but with Annie's help and Matthew Lock's tact, the military contract was retained.

He appeared now from Savile Row, hesitating in the open doorway looking ruffled, polished shoes on sockless feet. He held out *The Times* folded to page four where the newspaper reported major events.

"We're at war," he said. "It's official."

The young men looked at each other. The armed forces would take care of the fighting, surely...Leave it to the professionals. They looked at their patron in confusion.

"The job we're doing," said Matthew Lock, "is considered essential war work."

When Harry came back from the baker's next morning, he carried an armful of newspapers for them to read over breakfast.

"Why so many?" Maudie was soothing the baby's back after his feed.

"I want to know what's going on," said Harry. He leaned towards his son's face peeping over Maudie's shoulder and stroked a shammy-soft cheek. "They're all biased one way or another so I thought we'd get a better idea if we read the lot."

Maudie tucked Ace into his basket, poured tea and began reading a war poem in *The Times*. David grabbed the *Daily Mirror* to look at photographs of mobilising troops, and Harry read the *Manchester Guardian*'s prediction that the country was facing 'the greatest calamity that anyone living has known.' Every day through August they read at least one newspaper together with their morning bagels. The *Daily Mail* gave them tips on Housekeeping for Wartime, and the *Daily Express* reported a demonstration outside the German Embassy, where the hostile crowd were said to be 'groaning and hissing'.

"Listen to this," said Harry, wiping his mouth. "*The Chronicle* says that the stories published throughout the war might not give readers the full picture."

"Why not? Why would they say that?" David was often puzzled by the news.

"Because," said Harry, "and I quote: 'a newspaper's duty is to give news, but at times of war it has a patriotic duty as well. It must give no news which would convey information or advantage to the adversary.'"

While Harry was reading, Maudie detected a minute swell of pride in his voice, and at that moment she knew with unpleasant certainty that he would enlist. Harry would be unstoppable, and she'd stand by him because, if she were a man, she'd choose the same option. The thought surprised her.

September 1914

The war was predicted to be over by Christmas, and the newsreels showed thousands of eager men answering the call to arms. In London, a recruiting office was opened to raise a platoon of City workers, and within a week sixteen hundred men had enlisted to form the Stockbrokers Battalion. All over the country, complete battalions were being created out of footballers, miners and tramway employees. Harry sat upright in the flickering darkness, staring into the chirpy young faces of these men. He should be among them. Making uniforms wasn't enough. He wanted to be wearing khaki. He turned to David, who nodded as though he'd heard every thought.

On the way to the recruiting station at Somerset House they saluted one of Kitchener's 'Be a Man and Enlist Now!' posters pasted to a wall. Suddenly David was smacking his cheeks sharply and groaning.

"We've fallen for the propaganda."

"We have," said Harry. "But we also know it's the right thing to do – don't we?"

David kept staring at the poster.

"We're showing our resistance," said Harry.

"Right," said David. "But it's France that's being attacked."

"England next. Our parents brought us to a good place and we don't want to see it taken over."

"Okay, okay. I just wanted to check on my manliness."

"You're a sissy if I catch you." Harry raced him round a lamp post before they crossed the Strand to join a heady scrum of volunteers queuing for physicals.

Before the week was over they'd been given travel warrants to an army camp in Hampshire. Harry stared at the thick khaki coat he was making; he might soon be the soldier wearing it. He looked across the table at Maudie, absorbed in the toque she was making, banding the crown with lace. He picked up the recruitment papers that detailed their posting into a new battalion of the London Regiment; the tradesmen of the city were going to be turned into a fighting force.

"We'll be known as the London Rifle Brigade," he said.

Maudie was silent. She arranged the hat on her head and stood looking at the effect in a mirror. He watched her adjust the high collar of her slim-cut dress, and noticed how the filmy cloth draped over her still-plump belly. He dropped the army papers and went to her, burying himself in her arms.

"How can I leave you?" he whispered.

"Remember what you told me," she said. "A courageous man is someone who's afraid of doing his duty, but does it anyway."

"Did I say that? I must be barmy."

"No, my darling, you were revealing yourself. Anyway, isn't the war supposed to be over long before the baby's first birthday?"

"Yes, of course. The war will be over before we've finished training."

They looked into each other's eyes and knew that both were supporting a myth.

Chapter Three

France, 16th July 1916

Writing in his canvas-bound journal, Corporal White recorded a '*pathetic incident*' with copperplate precision.

> *I was ordered to stand arms at 2.45am, parade at 3am. We formed up on parade to hear one of our men being shot. We did not see him, but we heard the report of the rifles at 3.45am. The CO then came and read out to us the verdict of the court martial: guilty of misbehaving before the enemy in such a manner as to show cowardice.*

Corporal White chewed on the end of his pen before adding, *"I must say it had a very depressing effect on the whole battalion."*

London, 20th August 1916

Maudie took the embossed military letter from the postman, concentrating all her attention on his cap with its little peak of lacquered leather. She stood in the doorway, swaying slightly as her eyes traced and retraced the narrow band of piping round the blue crown of the hat.

"Best sit down, Miss."

Maudie backed into the hallway and sat abruptly on an upright chair, staring straight ahead.

The postman inclined his head. "Is anyone with you?"

Maudie nodded. She wanted him to be gone. She had to know.

She could feel the blood leaving her hands as she opened the envelope, and with icy fingers she withdrew a single sheet of paper. Her eyes skittered over the words, unseeing. She tried again, focusing on the first line addressing her as Madam; swinging to the illegible signature of an officer in charge of infantry records. A dreadful curiosity propelled her to read the full paragraph.

> *I am directed to inform you that a report has been received from the War Office to the effect that Private Harald Hooker was sentenced after trial by court martial to suffer death by being shot for cowardice, and the sentence was duly executed on 16th July 1916. I am, Madam, your obedient servant…*

"Coward?" The word ricocheted through the narrow hallway and slammed into her little son, standing unremembered in the shadows. He was there when his mother slid to the floor.

Chapter Four

Soho, 20th August 1916

Sitting beside his mother's unconscious body in the hallway, Ace lifted one of her cold hands to his face and kissed it fiercely.

"Wake up, Mummy." When Maudie opened her eyes he clapped his hands. He was two years old.

Maudie gave him a dazed smile before remembering. She sat up and reached for him, choking back a knot of chyme catapulting from the pit of her stomach. She made for the stairs with Ace in her arms, retching into the sink on the landing as the workroom door opened. Annie lifted Ace from her grasp and took him inside. Maudie followed, incoherent.

Her body shook with convulsions in the circle of Annie's arms. Ace slurped milk and practised the new word his mother had shouted in the hallway. "*Coward*," he said, in a conversational tone, and Maudie pulled away from Annie shouting "No!" In the background, Ace filed it away as a bad new word while Annie pushed Maudie into the sagging armchair and made her swallow brandy. Maudie looked up at Annie's hovering face pursed with anxiety, and wished her friend wasn't alone to cope with the weight of it all. She reached to touch the ghost-pale face as Annie sank to the floor beside her, ancient at the age of seventeen.

Matthew Lock found them in this tableau of collapse when he arrived to collect his grandson for an outing. He took them all back to Savile Row, giving Maudie a sleeping draught before he read her official letter. He thought of his small attempt to protect Harry and

David from enlisting, but Kitchener's recruitment campaign had been irresistible to at least three million young men. One of them was his son-in-law, now dead; deliberately killed by his own side during the slaughter on the Somme. His head felt so heavy he buried it in his arms.

Maudie's grief fuelled a manic energy. Orders for military hats were still urgent, and with Annie's help she doubled her output of forage-caps for the infantry while Ace sat on the floor making button towers. When she wasn't making hats, she was in bed re-reading Harry's letters; tracing the arc of his destructive journey into war. His early letters from the army camp at Winchester were upbeat and funny. Making soldiers out of tailors, cobblers, watch-makers and barbers was the stuff of farce, and she still smiled at his account of their bungling first day with rifles on the range, and his sketch of the clown who shot off his big toe.

While Harry and David were learning to shoot, Maudie was gradually taking over the whole workroom for millinery and Annie started training to be a hat maker. They worked together with ease, and it seemed logical for Annie to sleep in her brother's messy bedroom next door when they worked late into the night. She lived with her father above the stables at number two-and-a-half Wardour Mews, sharing the poky flat with three younger siblings and a housekeeper.

"Please let me," said Annie when her father hesitated at Maudie's suggestion. "I've never slept in a room of my own."

"I'll miss you," he said, almost to himself. A runaway horse had felled his wife and the war had lured his son. Now Annie was leaving.

"I'll only be round the corner," she told him as she packed her belongings.

Maudie knew that since his wife's death when Annie was twelve, Aaron had been overprotective of his eldest daughter. She reminded him that in situations like this, she'd heard him reflect on the wisdom of his Polish bubbe: 'First you give them roots; then wings.'

After ten months Maudie had been allowed to visit Harry before his regiment left for France. She travelled to the army camp in a close-fitting costume belted at the hip, with high-heeled shoes and a feathered hat. Her soldier husband had already rented a room in town for the night, and he thrilled her with his passion. When she finally caught her breath, Maudie gave him a mischievous look. "*What* have they been training you for?"

The letter he wrote on the voyage from Southampton was from a boyish adventurer, high on adrenalin, larking about with boisterous pals. She'd thought at the time she could smell salt-spray on the paper, but now when she pressed the page to her nose, only a void filled her nostrils.

The first letter from a frontline trench came a month later, in August 1915. His droll observations of daily life beside a war zone latrine did not fool Maudie. She could tell he was shaken, and sweat marks from her fingers stained the pages. Ace became clinging and the workload engulfed her as she lost focus. Noticing the change, her father suggested taking his grandson with him on neighbourhood visits. Often they went to see Aaron's horses. The two men had become friends since the contentious wedding; both were widowers in their late forties, with the generosity and compassion of resourceful men. They came from different backgrounds, but they shared the same outlook, and Ace grew up adoring them. Unexpectedly, he also developed an intense attachment to his paternal grandparents, stretching out eager arms as soon as they came into his orbit. The magnetic pull was mutual; having felt diminished by Harry's marriage to Maudie, the Hookers were caught off-guard when Ace was born. They hadn't thought they could accept him, but one glimpse at the familiar shape of his sloping eyes and they claimed him unconditionally. All the love and approval withheld from Harry was now channelled into this golden boy.

Maudie wrote, describing the bond developing between their son and Harry's parents. She knew he'd be glad, though he didn't mention it in any of his sombre letters from the Somme; the ones she could hardly bear to read. Now she poured over them obsessively, holding them to her heart, keeping him close. She wasn't looking for clues; she knew the war had unhinged him. He'd written to her in September after taking part in the Battle of Loos. He was in a hospital in France, diagnosed with shell shock, and she read the letter with raggedy breath.

"*I'm doing my duty and it's killing me,*" he wrote in a shaky hand. "*I don't know why I'm here in this manmade Hell where death is the only way out. I try to sleep but when I close my eyes the bed fills with bodies. There's no space for me to breathe, let alone sleep.*" At the bottom of the page he'd scribbled, "*What remains is my love for you which is a constant. This is what keeps me alive my darling wife.*"

Harry's mental decline coincided with Maudie's millinery ascent. And when *Vogue* magazine illustrated some of her hats in their autumn 1915 issue, she nearly buckled; the horrors of war were being offset by heightened levels of frivolity, and she was part of it. Suddenly a Maud Lock Original had become an essential item in a sophisticate's wardrobe. Her designs were witty and ironic, with military elements echoing in her helmet-shaped cloches and tall toques, spiky with regimental hussar feathers. Ideas flowed, and with a few deft sketches Maudie conveyed enough for Annie to grasp the essentials for shaping and blocking a hat.

A letter from David sent them into a spin: expect Harry, he said. He'd recovered his sight and would be given home leave when he left hospital. Maudie had no idea blindness was a symptom of shell shock. She hadn't seen Harry since he'd gone to war. There was a refrain inside her about repairing his broken spirit with her love, but she already sensed a gulf in her understanding of his condition.

While she and Annie pounded woollen cloth in hot water to make felt for the *Vogue*-featured winter hats, Harry left hospital and went back to the trenches.

"I couldn't leave David to fight without me," he wrote. Maudie crushed the letter into a ball before she could stop herself. When she smoothed it out, she felt the pressure dents from his pen on the page.

"I hate this futile war," she read. *"It makes me unreliable when I see good men blown to bits in these bloody battles for one inch of enemy territory."* Several sentences were blacked out by the army censor, but Maudie got the gist: Harry was exhausted.

The grapevine outside the workroom window began to bud. It was time to choose fabric for the summer cloches. Maudie bought fine straw with a linen-look weave that was made from sisal, and while they went into production, Annie's little sisters darted in and out, running errands and helping to look after Ace. He was a good-natured little boy, and they only had to make him a playtent of khaki cloth and hat trimmings draped over a chair to keep him crooning through the afternoons.

Harry's last letter from the Somme came in July 1916, when grapes were forming on the Meard Street vine. It was a scribbled note ending in many kisses:

"Paddling in the trench, waiting for our rum ration before the next assault. Stretcher-bearers collecting the wounded. David is with me."

September 1916

Maudie glanced at the clock: 2am. She listened for a moment to the snuffles of her son's breathing before climbing out of bed to inhale the smoky smell of his skin. She stroked his shiny small fists as she tucked him in, aware of a strange sensation; as though she was her own mother covering little Maudie. Was she experiencing the last memory of her touch? She padded into the living room to contemplate her mother's portrait, painted when she was twenty-five with fuzzy gold hair and a myopic smile. Maudie was two when she died of tuberculosis. After crying inconsolably for a week, she'd never cried again from loss. She didn't cry now, though her beloved man Harry was dead.

Maudie could see that Annie was jumpy and distracted – probably thinking about David in a trench without Harry, though she didn't want to ask. He hadn't written since Annie's letter about Maudie's expanding fame. She'd sent her brother a sheet from the fashion magazine featuring the hats, and told Maudie she chattered on for pages before wondering if she was being tactless. She promised she wouldn't make a fuss about vacating David's room at Meard Street when he came back.

Twelve days after the news of Harry's death, Annie's fat letter came back; returned unopened, defaced by a printed message. Maudie watched her blink several times as though to clear her vision. She wouldn't be able to bear what she read. The dumb words would float, then sharpen. There'd be no mistake even though, in the chaos of the battlefront, it had arrived ahead of the official condolence for the loss of a brave man. Maudie had passed her the letter and seen the words stamped on the envelope: Killed in Action.

Overnight, a strand of Annie's rich brown hair turned white.

In the hollow days that followed, whenever Maudie glanced across the room at Annie, the silver streak had a startling impact. The visible shock-effect and her effortless tears seemed admirable to Maudie, the dry-eyed mourner, whose hair moulted privately all over her pillow. She worked assiduously, scorched with envy that Annie's family knew the details of what had happened to David. The compassionate letter that followed, from the captain of his company – *Harry's company too!* – stressed that David had died fighting in the battle for Mametz Wood. *Was Harry with him then?* The captain said David was buried near the wood "in a soldier's grave where he fell." *Where was Harry buried when he fell?* And the captain sent comforting words for them to cling to: "We all honour him and trust that you will feel some consolation in remembering this."

Where are MY comforting words? Maudie howled in silence as she bent to unwelcome work, veiling a hat in black lace for a war widow.

CHAPTER FIVE

France, October 1916

In a billet three miles behind the front line, an army chaplain bent reluctantly to his work. Condolence letters were Wilfred Goodfellow's pastoral concern, but each one was uniquely painful to write. The *Shot at Dawn* executions were the most dispiriting. He'd known this particular soldier and was anguished that any man who'd volunteered to fight could meet his death before a firing squad of his own comrades. In moments like these he despaired of finding suitable words. He turned to Second Lieutenant John Flower for a briefing, and regarded his abstract pacing among the huddled shapes of men who'd simply dropped to the floor in deep sleep. The London Regiment was resting in requisitioned farm buildings after a week of continuous fighting. Although the second lieutenant was a walking wreck, his unlikely malachite eyes still flashed from his grimy face. Goodfellow knew Flower hadn't been allowed to speak for Private Harry Hooker at his court-martial, and was outraged by the arbitrary execution a day later of a man under his command.

He imagined the soldier was struggling under the weight of army censorship, and it was some time before the chaplain was able to attract his attention.

"I'm sorry Goodfellow," he said. "I'm being no help at all." Flower scratched the thick mat of his filthy blond hair before sitting heavily beside the chaplain. "My God, I'm knackered!" He sighed as the bench groaned under his weight. " Would you add my deepest regrets?" He massaged his neck muscles with battered fingers as though trying to marshal his thoughts.

"His wife should be told he was an exceptional soldier who inspired others with his courage."

The chaplain nodded and began writing as Flower's eyes glazed over.

"What I'd like to do," he said, "would be to visit the widow when this damned war's over." He staggered to his feet and started pacing again among his spent men.

"Listen, Goodfellow," said Flower. "I want to tell her what I couldn't say at Hooker's court-martial."

Chapter Six

Soho 1920

The loose square mile of Soho was the world to Ace. Maudie let him roam freely in the red-light district of London because there was always someone who knew where he was. He was six years old, tall for his age, with Harry's dark blue sloping eyes and a thicket of crow-black hair. He moved fast, with a darting wired energy, and couldn't sit still without jiggling a leg. He was taken under the collective wing of his neighbours because he'd lost his father in the war.

His school in Peter Street was five minutes from home, in a cul-de-sac off Berwick Street market. In summer he might make a detour into the market to wangle a peach in exchange for delivering a message, but mostly he couldn't wait to get to school. When Ace started there as a new boy, Maudie went with him every day for a week, guiding him to the school gate and crossing the playground to the boys' entrance. On the first day of term, Mr Fiber the headmaster handed Ace a perfect strawberry and asked him to draw the fruit before eating it. Ace barely noticed his mother leaving.

She was at the gate when he came out of school, and he bounded towards her, eyes wide. He told her everything he could remember while she led him to *Vogue's* office in Brewer Street; she'd finished making her latest cloche and the magazine wanted to photograph a fashion model wearing it. Ace carried the tissue-wrapped hat as they walked along the street of Italian shops; sacks of pasta sagged in doorways, jagged chunks of Parmesan filled the windows, and greetings of *buona sera* sailed towards passers-by. He practised the phrase until it sounded authentic, and on the way back tried it out on staff at Serena Stores and was rewarded with a cherry liqueur bonbon wrapped in gold paper.

"That's the sort of bitter chocolate your bubbe would like," said Maudie, and Ace stuffed it in his pocket. He hated dark chocolate.

After school next day they went to see Uncle Aaron, who shared the cobbled yard with a carpenter, a dairyman and a cow called Beryl. Aaron was unharnessing his horse after a day of deliveries.

"I was hoping you'd come," he said. "I could do with your help."

Ace felt indispensable at the stables – in-dis-pens-able, Aaron had taught him – and he knew what was required. He took hold of the halter and laid the flat of his hand on Angel's sweaty nose to calm her while his uncle rubbed her down and prepared a feed. Ace borrowed a knife to cut up an apple, writhing at the soft rubbery lips tickling his open palm where he laid the slices. He listened to Maudie talking to Aaron, and watched the easy way she stood in the mucky yard, wearing a pretty frock and not minding a bit about manure and wood shavings sticking to her summer shoes, or flies landing on her face.

"Shall we go and see Bubbe and Zeidy tomorrow?" she asked as they swung home hand in hand.

Ace stared up at her. He usually went to see his grandparents by himself. They lived just round the corner from home, where they welcomed him with strange adventure stories and special sweet food. When his mother came too, their voices were snappy and the stories weren't fun.

When he didn't answer, Maudie said, "The best thing is for me to show you the way from school; then you can go when you want."

He didn't know she was providing him with a structure; establishing a pattern she hoped he would follow. She never insisted on these visits, but she always asked for the story of his day when he got home, and stopped whatever she was doing to give him her undivided attention. She listened, and Ace learned how to tell a story to extend the moment. It soothed him to see her long-fingered hands at rest.

On his first schoolboy visit to his grandparents by himself, Ace found Zeidy in his usual place – cross-legged on his worktable. He climbed up and sat beside him, crossing his legs in imitation of the master tailor. It seemed the natural thing to do, and his grandfather's flinty face softened as he finished hand-stitching a woollen coat. He worked till ten every night except Saturday, but he always had time for his grandson. Ace sat beside him, absorbing the humid atmosphere. For at least five minutes he was engrossed in watching a young apprentice unpicking basting threads with a bodkin, and the presser sliding tailor's soap over a coat seam before hefting a fourteen-pound iron. He stared at the volume of sweat pouring down the man's singlet as he stood over the smoking sleeveboard.

Bubbe appeared in her apron, seeming to gauge when Ace was about to grow fidgety. She plucked her grandson from the table into a tight embrace before whisking him into the kitchen for a bowl of noodle soup. He was breathless from the hug, but her smell of honey and spices gave him an appetite. The three-room flat steamed with activity. Traders came and went all day, and while Ace tried to help his grandmother roll pastry thin enough for an apple strudel, the machinist arrived for a stint of piecework and the shop boy staggered off to Savile Row with an armful of coats protected by a black wrapper.

A pedlar hesitated at the door as sweet cooking smells drifted through the flat. He came often, a melancholy man in a tragic suit with a case of buttons and sewing silk. Ace's grandparents always bought something because they'd known him when he had a trimmings shop in Berwick Street, before illness diminished him. Zeidy carefully unfolded his legs and stepped from the table to shake the man's hand, and Bubbe handed him a mug of tea with a piece of freshly-baked strudel. Ace watched, considering the life of a pedlar when he grew up.

Maudie was making fishcakes for their supper when he came home. She sat down at the kitchen table, wiping mashed potato from her fingers while he gave her an elaborate account of the pedlar's visit. She smiled at the description.

"That must be Mr Budd. Did he have a beard?"

"Yes!" Ace jumped about. "I forgot to say he was The Whiskered Gentleman." He was remembering the buttonholer's words, announcing the pedlar's arrival to his grandfather.

"The whiskered Mr Budd ran the shop where I used to buy my hat trimmings," she said. Ace waited for more.

"The shop was called Budd Brothers, and they sold the best ribbons and lace, but his brother died and Mr Budd couldn't manage the shop on his own."

"Why?" He scooped a finger of fishcake mixture from the pot.

"A pertinent question, my ill-mannered son," she said, slapping his hand. " I think he was so unhappy about his brother dying that it made him ill. He just stopped working, so he lost all his customers and eventually lost the shop when he couldn't pay the rent anymore. Your grandparents tried to help him, but Mr Budd was deranged."

A new word. Ace opened his mouth to ask for an explanation, but his mother's face had changed: she was wearing her uncooked currant-bun look. Her eyes had gone dark and tiny in a face that was doughy and shapeless. Nothing like his mother's lovely features. He pressed his lips together; he hated the way she sometimes disappeared inside herself. His legs knocked against the table until her smoky eyes swam back into focus.

"Being deranged is a kind of madness," she said. "Things can happen in a person's life that make them behave in peculiar ways. Mr Budd was hurt inside when his brother died, and it deranged him. Your father was upset by seeing friends die in the war, and that deranged him."

Ace yawned. He didn't want to be a pedlar when he grew up, and his father was just the grainy photograph on the living room wall showing a man with scary eyebrows.

"Mr B the Bear's hungry." He waggled the paw of his hug-squashed toy with its lopsided face and lugubrious expression. 'Loo-goo-bri-as' was a favourite word.

Because Ace felt at home anywhere in Soho, a dark alleyway like Walker's Court was just a place close to school. Curiosity led him through it one aimless afternoon and he came across a smart young woman sobbing loudly in a doorway. He stood transfixed by the ruin of her heavy eye makeup.

"What d'you think you're staring at?" she snarled, and Ace said, "Please don't cry." His voice was like a balm and she stopped with a hiccup and blew her nose copiously.

"Where do you come from?" she said, fumbling in her purse for a powder compact. She snapped it open and shrieked as she looked in the mirror.

"I live in Meard Street." Ace dug in his pockets as though to find some identity and his right hand closed over the cherry chocolate from Serena Stores. He pulled it out and offered it to her.

"Sweets from a stranger!" she said. "You're a cutie aren't you? What's your name?"

"Ace Hooker." He watched as she dabbed mascara from her cheeks and applied crimson lipstick to her mobile mouth.

"Well, that's a flash Harry name for a little kid, ain't it?"

Ace beamed. "That's my other name."

"Flash Harry's your other name? Cor blimey, Ace!" She erupted with wheezy laughter and lit a cigarette. "My name's Poppy and I'm pleased to meet you." She held out a hand and he saw matching crimson nails peeping through her white lace gloves. Everything about her was fascinating, and he was about to ask what had made her cry when a man walked by, retraced his steps and stood blatantly in front of her.

"Hop it, Ace," she hissed. "I'm busy now. See you another day."

He ran home to tell his mother about Poppy. He was earlier than usual and she hadn't finished an order. "I'm so sorry, Ace," she said, distracted. "I can't stop. She'll be here in half an hour." When he sighed dramatically, his mother pulled him into a hug.

"I believe your Mr B has seen those little pastries Bubbe made. Do you know where they are?" Ace ducked from her grasp and made for the kitchen to organise tea for his woolly chum.

Maudie glanced at the clock and grimaced at the unfinished hat. She and Annie spent all their work hours making cloches; it was becoming the iconic hat of the Twenties, and Maudie's art deco designs were in demand. They were also time-consuming to make, being subtle constructions of zigzag seaming. She looked along the table to Annie's workspace where a heap of felt in soft autumn shades was neatly stacked beside her millinery equipment. She'd learned fast to shape and block a hat; Maudie felt lucky to be working with a talented person who was also her best friend. As she sewed, she wondered how Annie was getting on with the client who'd required a home visit for her hat-fitting. She listened to Ace in the kitchen, chattering to his bear, and knew she had a few minutes left before he'd be insisting on her attention. St Anne's clock chimed the hour as she fastened a diamond clip to the side of the finished cloche. She swivelled the hat on one finger, approving the pattern of jigsaw shapes she'd designed to echo the bias-cut dress it would be worn with. She rubbed her eyes and smoothed her hair, now shaped into a sleek bob that emphasised the beauty of her bone structure.

The doorbell rang as she went to fetch Ace, and he clattered down the stairs to let in the hat client. A grand lady in red stepped forward to give him a strong handshake, and in surprise, he introduced her to his bear. She held the proffered sugary paw in both hands and said it was a rare pleasure.

"Ace!" called his mother, and he hurried the red lady up the stairs.

"It was Mr B," he said, rolling his eyes. "He wanted to say hallo."

"He was most insistent," agreed the client, peeling off sticky gloves before touching the new hat.

"Did Mr B know he was meeting Lady Plumb?" said Maudie as she adjusted the cloche on her client's sleek head.

"I expect so." Ace was thoughtful. "He's quite par-tic-u-lar."

"Me too," said her ladyship. "I wouldn't shake hands with any old bear."

In bed that night, he remembered Poppy. His story at suppertime had been all about the magic experiment at school; Mr Fiber moving nuts and bolts over the refectory table without ever touching them. "His hand was *under* the table all the time," said Ace. "He was using a …" His mother looked expectant and Ace willed himself to remember the name. " Mag-net!" he said in a rush, and she kissed him for being clever.

Had he forgotten to tell her about Poppy? He told his mother everything. He was stirred by a dark thought: Poppy was his first secret.

Chapter Seven

Having a secret made Ace more alert. It made him aware that his grandparents had one too. They acted like deaf people if his mother mentioned Harry. But Harry was his father, and though he'd never bothered to ask before, now he wanted to know about the deranged man with wild eyebrows.

He'd made friends at school with an inquisitive French boy who worked in his father's tavern in Dean Street, and Pierre asked what his father did.

"Oh, he's dead," said Ace.

"Why?" Pierre made goggle eyes.

"In the war." Ace screwed up his face to recall what his mother had said. "He was killed in France."

"My country!" Pierre's shiny fair hair fanned out as he kicked a ball against the playground wall. "Is he buried there? Is he a hero?"

"Don't know," said Ace.

"You know what a war hero is, don't you?" Pierre was about to be scathing, but he couldn't help explaining. "It's when you do brave things. In a war," he added helpfully "you might kill hundreds and hundreds of men all by yourself."

Ace fidgeted with the ball. "I know *that.*" He sifted his memory for a glimpse of his father alive, but nothing came. " He went to war when I was a baby."

He sounded so bleak that Pierre grabbed him by the arm and tugged him to the school gate. He was a small-boned boy with a persuasive sinewy strength. "Come home with me," he said. "Papa will give us bottles of ginger pop if we pick up empties for him."

Ace had never tasted ginger pop, but he knew about collecting glasses. He'd helped out at the Blue Posts in Berwick Street after meeting the publican at his grandfather's. They were old friends from Poland, and Mr Kezelman had shaken hands with Ace and said "Call me Mr K," not knowing the boy's taste for syllabled words. Ace had liked the malty smell of the empty beer glasses, and Mr K gave him a penny and thanked him for being so quick and unobtrusive. He was running a busy bar, but Ace wouldn't leave until Mr K explained the meaning of un-ob-troo-siv.

'Home' for Pierre was the flat where he was born above the Dean Street Tavern, and everything about his life intrigued Ace. Here were strange individuals drinking absinthe at a bar presided over by a jovial man with the bushiest moustache he'd ever seen: Papa Pierre. His mother was jolly too, with the biggest bosom ever, and he watched closely as her hairy husband hugged her for bringing him a steaming dish of mussels. Papa Pierre's laugh rumbled from the depths of his belly, and his thick fingers were surprisingly gentle as he ran them through his son's fine hair. When he planted a paternal kiss on Pierre's head, Ace touched the top of his own.

Crossing Old Compton Street on the way home, he saw his mother. She seemed to be hypnotised by a display of snuff powders in the tobacconist's window, her head pressed against the glass. He called out and she turned to him with fog-filled eyes.

"What's that?" He touched the letter in her hand as Maudie steadied herself against the shopfront.

"John Flower's in London!"

Ace stared at her; the name meant nothing to him.

"Second Lieutenant John Flower. He was in the war with your father." Maudie's eyes had cleared. "He's coming to tell us what happened." She swooped him up and danced a jig on the pavement. Ace forgot to struggle because he was engrossed with his mother's news; a man from the war was coming, a man who would tell him his father was a *hero*.

"When's he coming?" Ace escaped from her arms, and Maudie leaned against the shop window, fanning her face with the letter.

"Soon I think." She tried to smooth his spiky wired hair. "Look at your neck," she said. "I was coming to fetch you from Pierre's to go to the baths. You must have forgotten it was Friday."

"Who told you I was at Pierre's?"

"Annie saw you together. When I came downstairs to find you, the postman was delivering John Flower's letter. I'd stopped to take a peak at it when you saw me."

"You looked a bit queer," said Ace.

"I *felt* queer. It's been four years." She scanned the letter. "There's an address I'm to write to if I want to meet him."

"You DO want to meet him." Ace examined her face and decided John Flower would want to hug his mother if he saw that smile. He touched the top of his head again.

With her son in a dreamy mood, Maudie had no trouble persuading Ace to have his weekly bath at Marshall Street. Like most Soho residents, they didn't have a bathroom at home or a copper in the kitchen, so they took baskets of washing to launder as well as a clean towel for the sixpenny hot bath. Maudie took a translucent bar of Pears Soap for herself and a loofah to scrub Ace. She once paid half price for the cold bath option when clients still owed her for hats, but after Ace's echoing screams, she borrowed from her father next time she was short. She knew Matthew Lock loved helping her, but Maudie was trying to be independent of his generosity. Borrowing money from her father for a bath was provocative because he wanted to install a bathroom for her at Meard Street. It was a luxury she longed for and she knew she'd agree eventually.

The laundry behind the baths was a lively social scene. Women took flasks of tea and sandwiches for a convivial afternoon with their washing, and Maudie and Annie, taking laundry turns each week, caught up with the gossip while they fed their bed linen through the mangle. At the time, memorials were being established on the Somme battlefield to honour the dead, and in preparation for Armistice Day 1920, there was talk of a local memorial to commemorate Londoners killed in battle.

"Only the heroes, mind," emphasised a heavy woman cloaked in black.

It was here, while Annie was methodically folding sheets, that she first heard of *Shot at Dawn* executions, and the spicy rumour that one of the British soldiers shot for cowardice in the war was a Soho man. She couldn't bring herself to tell Maudie that her neighbours were speculating on the identity of the shamed widow among them.

Maudie dithered over John Flower's letter. When the chaplain wrote in 1916 telling her of the second lieutenant's wish to talk to her after the war, she was ravenous for anything he could tell her of Harry's death. The war ended, and with no word from John Flower she assumed he was dead too, and she stopped expecting his letter. She'd already built up an acceptable story for herself to account for Harry's execution. She'd read all she could find about shell shock, and come to the conclusion that the condition was misunderstood and trivialised. She'd known from her husband's letters that he'd been in a state of mental exhaustion; she saw him as a brave man who'd been sabotaged by his nervous system. He'd temporarily gone blind, and then irretrievably lost his way. She didn't know if he'd actually run away or refused to climb out of the trenches to fight; what she did know was that her husband had been regarded as a burden on the battlefield. Over time it grew obvious to her: soldiers who became incapable of fighting had to be removed from the frontline, and if they didn't rally after a short rest in hospital, they were expendable. The crude army solution was to place them in front of a firing squad of their own comrades to teach everyone a lesson.

Maudie had never doubted the courage of Harry's heart, but she was afraid. John Flower might tell her something disturbing; something that wouldn't fit the story she'd developed for herself over four years.

There was a missing piece: what happened while Harry was crouched in a trench, waiting for the pre-assault rum ration with his cousin David?

They'd been watching stretcher-bearers, Harry had written, and Maudie imagined them lifting fallen men from the mud, hauling them off to casualty stations and coming back for more; there were always more. At this point Maudie's narrative would stutter to a halt. Was she trying to protect herself from what happened next?

She rummaged through her bureau for writing paper and took out Chaplain Goodfellow's condolence letter. Maudie remembered how she'd sat on a window seat in the workroom to read it. Harry had been dead four months and she'd stared out at the grey sky, the leafless brown vine, and the world without her husband in it. Her immediate response had been to cut off the curls he'd loved and shape her shock-thinned hair into a severe bob.

The letter had been a comfort – the first kind words from a military source. The army chaplain had mentioned Private Hooker's 'courage' and assured Maudie that Second Lieutenant John Flower, as leader of Harry's section on the fatal day, wanted to give his account of her 'exceptional' husband. How she'd held on to those two complimentary words, as a talisman against any lurking doubt. No need to fear ghosts, she told herself. This man Flower had positive things to say; he would explain why David had died heroically while Harry was despatched by a British bullet.

After posting her reply agreeing to meet him at the Waldorf

Hotel, she asked Annie, as her best friend and David's sister, what she should tell Harry's parents.

Annie looked up from shaping a hat. "You think they'll censor you for meeting a man for tea?"

"I hadn't thought of that, you monkey. No, I thought they might want to meet him."

"Why would they want to do that?" Annie's voice was sharp. "They never talk about Harry – they've eliminated him." She swept expressive hands away from her, palms down, obliterating.

"But John Flower might be able to help them. He might be able to restore honour to their boy."

Annie looked sceptical. "You and I know Harry deserves honour – we know it in our bones, don't we? But your in-laws, well!" Annie tickled her upturned nose with a feather and sneezed. "No harm in telling them he's here, I suppose, but they may be resentful." She assembled a fan of small feathers to decorate the side of a hat and looked mischievously at Maudie.

"Introduce him to ME – I'm mad keen to meet him. I hope he's dashing."

"He might be in a wheelchair for all we know," said Maudie.

"Was he wounded? He didn't say in his letter, did he?"

"The war's been over for two years. He could have been recovering in a hospital all that time."

After a moment, Annie said, "Well, I still want to meet him. Even if he's in a wheelchair, I think he's going to be dishy."

Maudie looked at her friend. At twenty-one, Annie's plain small features had acquired a beguiling elfin quality. Her long neck was accentuated by bobbed chestnut hair, and the dramatic streak of silver dating from her brother's death had become an enviable fashion highlight. By comparison, Maudie felt dull, and old at twenty-nine. She'd found that being a war widow carried social obligations of respectability, although her behaviour since Harry's death had been impeccable. She couldn't imagine another man in her life, but she'd surprised herself at the thought of tea with John Flower; she detected a flicker of interest in him as a man.

Maudie's conciliatory visit to Harry's parents with John Flower's letter stirred their four-year silence about the war. She took Ace with her to soften their response, but her in-laws were affronted by the very mention of Harry's death.

"Leave him be," warned his mother.

Maudie breathed deeply to dissolve her irritation. "At least read the letter. You think Harry was guilty of a crime, but this man wants to explain why Harry's life ended as it did. I believe he'll take away the shame. He'll…"

Samuel Hooker held up a silencing hand.

"You *believe*," he said. "Let me remind you Harry was judged by the professional expertise of the British Army." His voice was as stiff as his posture.

"But don't you want to know what the judgement was for?" Maudie's voice rose with agitation.

"He was convicted of a military offence that carried the death penalty." Samuel Hooker rubbed his brow as though to remove the deep furrows. "The details are irrelevant."

"Irrelevant?" Maudie jumped to her feet. She saw that he was struggling to compose himself and sat down again. "Yes, irrelevant in one sense because Harry was shell-shocked and probably unaware of his actions."

She saw the Hookers shudder as one. Of course, their understanding of shell shock would be associated with lily-livered soldiers of weak spirit.

Samuel Hooker moved to stand beside his wife, who was distracting Ace with an assortment of biscuits. "Whatever the case, the warrant was signed by Sir Douglas Haigh himself. He commanded the British forces – how could a second lieutenant know more than a general?"

"Because *he* was on the battlefield." Maudie glanced at Ace. "John Flower was with Harry and David – he saw what happened. He wants to tell us."

"My son is dead; nothing will bring him back." Samuel Hooker spoke with such pain in his voice that Maudie moved to comfort him. He drew back hissing: "Harry was a coward."

Ace stopped crunching biscuits. He'd heard that word before and it wasn't a good one. He stood in front of his grandfather.

"Zeidy," he said, looking up into glassy eyes, "why is my father dead?"

"Something happened to him in the war." His grandfather cleared his throat savagely. "Something happened."

The inquiring gaze of his grandson was too much for Samuel Hooker. Something about the blueblack density of the boy's eyes, the particular downward sloping shape of them, made him stumble from the room.

Ace watched him go. Zeidy had said Harry was a coward – was that his grandfather's secret? The meaning wasn't clear to him, but Pierre would know.

Chapter Eight

Ace collided with a substantial stranger when he ran out of the Tavern with his eyes shut. The man's hat fell off as he lurched towards the kerb, and instinctively, Ace grabbed hold of his coat to stop him crashing into the road. It was then he saw that the man had a bad leg.

"Sorry, Sir." He picked the hat out of the gutter and shook grit off the felt. The man took the hat, breathing heavily. Ace stared at him: green eyes that reminded him of the Tavern's peppermint liqueur, and eyebrows that were nearly white.

"You're stronger than you look," said the man. He glanced down at his lace-up shoes before striding past Ace into the bar.

Just before running blindly out of the Tavern, Ace had been talking to Pierre about words; about one word in particular.

"Your father was a coward?" Pierre's caramel eyes stretched with amazement.

"What does it *mean*?" Ace chewed on a drinking straw. It was ten minutes to opening time. They'd polished all the glasses and were sitting in their favourite hideaway corner with bottles of pear juice.

"Well..." Pierre was wary. "It's not a good word, I know that, but let's ask my papa."

"No!" Ace was adamant. "I want *you* to tell me what it means." He waited with thrumming legs while Pierre drained pear juice through his straw, looking quite important.

"A coward is someone who runs away."

Ace had braced himself for the worst, and it was the worst. He struggled for breath.

"He prob'ly ran away for a good reason," said Pierre. "If a wild dog was chasing after me, I'd run away!"

Were there wild dogs in the war? His father had run away from fighting – wasn't that it? Ace slid from his seat and rushed into the street.

John Flower took his pint to a corner table of the Tavern and slumped heavily into a chair. He was shaken by the fragility of his new leg; by his own fragility in fact. The leg itself was fine. It was the latest flexible design from the on-site workshops of a hospital in Surrey, where he'd convalesced while they custom-made one from a light metal alloy. They'd almost taught him to dance at the limb-training classes, but they hadn't shown him how to counter a small boy torpedo attack. He filled his mouth with amber ale and let it slide down his throat, reminding himself he was a civilian again, sitting in a London pub, savouring a drink.

On positive days, he almost felt lucky to have been injured at the end of the war. By 1918, with forty thousand British servicemen already minus a limb or two, a specialist hospital had opened in Roehampton to cater for veterans like John Flower, and the prostheses market moved from the peg-leg era into cutting edge technology. He left the hospital with a free artificial leg, plus a spare; his entitlement as a war-wounded soldier. He was thirty-one years old, his blond hair was still thick, and his new left leg was going to lead him astray.

He'd already had one intriguing encounter that afternoon while he zigzagged through the Soho streets on his way to the Tavern. He was practising a nonchalant stroll along an alleyway when a striking young woman in a red spotted frock stepped from a doorway and blocked his path. His left foot splayed in surprise.

"Hallo, Handsome – got a light?"

John Flower groaned inwardly at the old line, but her voice had a husky warmth and he reached in his pocket for matches. She slid a cigarette between her crimson lips and leaned towards the flame.

"So," she breathed, "you're a war hero."

"Losing a leg has nothing to do with courage," he said.

"Keep your blinkin' hair on." She was obviously used to navigating touchy ex-servicemen. "Getting *through* the war makes you a hero. My little brother was blown up in the first month. Eighteen years old, he was."

"I'm truly sorry." He touched her arm and she looked hopeful.

"Want to come upstairs?"

John Flower hesitated for a second, filled with an old longing. "Another time," he said, and because she looked so disappointed he pressed a pound note into her hand. "A down payment," he said.

As he walked away she called after him: "Ask for Poppy."

He finished his pint and ordered another, examining his response to Poppy. Had he stopped himself because he was meeting his uncle in half an hour, or… were fantasies about Maudie inhibiting him? Her reply to his letter was still in his pocket. She'd agreed to meet him, and he couldn't help reading into the generous curves of her handwriting. He imagined an exciting woman. He didn't care if his feelings were misplaced; he hungered for this meeting as though it was a romantic date. Two years as a hospital patient in France and England had blunted his desire for life. He'd been drenched in pain or stunned by drugs while injuries healed and doctors tried to save his shattered leg. When they cut it off above the knee, he begged them to cut off his head as well. He was heavily tranquillised and sent to the new limb hospital, where he gradually recovered his spirit and the will to walk.

And the will to live. He'd come to Soho to meet his Uncle Joe about work. He had a disability war pension, and advice to apply for an army desk job, but the very thought appalled him. John Flower was restless for a new occupation and Joe Flower the dance band leader had some ideas. His uncle chose the Tavern for its proximity to Archer Street, the open-air labour exchange for musicians.

John Flower had never played professionally, but he'd grown up mastering wind instruments in a musical household. While recuperating in the limb hospital, a physiotherapist asked him to recall a leg-free activity that gave him pleasure.

"Playing the saxophone," he'd said at once, weightless with joy that his arms were intact.

Uncle Joe sauntered into the Tavern, an older version of his nephew with thick silvered hair and the same blond eyebrows. John Flower loved this man for having insisted on a musical career regardless of parental threats. His father and grandfather had both been military men; they'd cajoled Joe's brother into the army, but Joe had run away with a trumpet at sixteen.

"This calls for champagne!" he announced, clasping both his nephew's hands. Papa Pierre beamed and bustled into action.

"What are we celebrating, Uncle?"

"Your new career." Joe was fizzing with energy. "What a piece of luck; on my way here I met an old friend who needs a saxophone player. Can you play jazz?" He paused. "Have you *heard* of jazz? The music scene's been getting lively while you've been out of action."

"Jazz..."

"Yes, black American folk music." Joe's body pitched about to a syncopated rhythm as he blew an imaginary trumpet. "While you were in hospital last year, a jazz band from New Orleans came over and played at the Albert Hall. They were jumping!"

"An American soldier in my regiment introduced me to jazz on his clarinet."

"Splendid. You're up to date then." Joe took off his coat as the champagne arrived at their table. "I didn't know you had Americans in the battalion."

"Plenty. They weren't allowed to enlist, but they did anyway, and this one smuggled his clarinet all the way to the Somme." John Flower leaned forward. "When he died, he left me the clarinet with a message."

"And the message read..." prompted Joe.

"*Play jazz.*"

"Well I'll be damned."

They toasted each other in champagne until the bottle was upturned in the ice bucket.

After bundling his uncle into a taxi home, Flower stood outside the Tavern, swaying. He intended making his way to the Aldwych. He was meeting Maudie in exactly one week and he wanted to establish that the Waldorf Hotel was still a good place for tea. He stumbled into Shaftesbury Avenue and turned right.

"Should have turned left," he mumbled as he turned right again into Rupert Street. He found himself walking through an alleyway, straight into the arms of Poppy. Was she really waiting for *him*? Not a very welcoming look, he noticed, but she took him firmly by the arm and encouraged him up a flight of stairs to the pitiful room she called her 'boudoir'.

He woke an hour later on her densely perfumed bed. Poppy was shaking him.

"Time's up, love." Her voice was brisk and Flower sat up, fully dressed and humiliated.

"You kipped through your down payment, so come back when you're sober." She ruffled his curly hair. "You're sweet; you were smiling in your sleep and all you wanted was a cuddle. Bye bye Mr Flower."

"Did I tell you my name?"

"No, love, I looked in your pocket, didn't I." Poppy's peals of laughter followed him down the stairs.

Feeling for his wallet, he took the last step awkwardly and

plunged through the doorway into the street, barging into a child walking by.

"Torpedo boy!" Flower tipped his hat to the slim woman in a sparkly cloche who'd stopped the child falling, and apologised to Ace before hurrying away on baffled legs.

Maudie watched him go. "Is that the man?"

Ace rubbed his bashed arm. "The Man with the Funny Leg." He'd told her the story earlier that evening on their way to Savile Row for supper with his grandfather. She'd said his description of the man's eyes was original.

Walking home, Ace said, "They were like peppermint liqueur, weren't they?"

"More like jewels to me," said Maudie.

Chapter Nine

One week later

Maudie was ten minutes late. She hesitated at the entrance to the hotel's glass-domed tearoom until the manager appeared at her elbow.

"A table for two in the name of Flower?" Her shoulders began to relax as he led her across the marble floor to a table where two men were in conversation. They both looked up at the heel-tap of her approach, and Maudie said, 'Oh!' before she could stop herself as the man with jewel eyes rose to introduce himself. His broad smile revealed haphazardly-spaced teeth.

"You're Maud Lock Hooker? How astonishing." He turned to his companion, who was holding a trumpet. "This beautiful lady was at the scene of a stupid accident I had last week. She came to the rescue and I've been dreaming about her ever since."

Maudie's scalp prickled. "Please don't exaggerate in case I take you seriously." Her laugh held a warning.

"You mean you had no idea she was the widow you'd arranged to meet? She could have been an old trout!" The trumpeter's shiny eyes darted over Maudie as she unfastened her wrapover coat from its single button. He played a sotto fanfare on his instrument, eyes still swivelling in her direction, registering cool grey eyes and a blue silk frock. "Lucky blighter!" he mouthed to Flower, as he shook spit from his trumpet and prepared to leave.

"This man," he told Maudie, gripping Flower by the arm, "is a most ungainly chap, but he blows the sax like a dream." He bowed and kissed her hand before flinging a cape over his shoulders and departing.

Maudie sank into the seat she was offered and shook out the flared skirt of the crepe-de-chine frock she'd made in four days. It steadied her to feel the fabric between her fingers. The coarseness of the trumpeter's behaviour receded as Flower took his seat. She sat up straight, reminding herself that Harry was the focus for this meeting; she must be imagining the sexual tension between them.

She listened to the animated buzz from tables around her, and to the stillness of her companion's silence. She was being watched by those eyes, and she tilted her head to mask the half-moons of darkness embedded under her own. Annie was right; all the nights of close work by gaslight were spoiling her looks.

"I owe you an apology," she said, explaining that she'd been delayed by a client's late arrival to collect a hat. Flower said nothing.

"I'm forgiven for being late, I hope!"

"Forgive *me*." He rubbed a hand over his face. "The surprise... Let's order; would you like Earl Grey?"

"No, Darjeeling please."

"Me too." The hovering waiter went off with the order and Flower repositioned his metal leg under the table while Maudie tucked stray wisps of hair back under her cloche.

"This isn't going to be easy," he said.

"No, it isn't," she agreed. "Shall we talk about something else first? Tell me how you know the precocious trumpeter."

"He's gross, isn't he? Max is a friend of my uncle's. He plays here, at the Waldorf."

"And you're a musician now?"

"Hoping to be, yes."

A waiter appeared with a balanced tray and set out individual pots of tea and jugs of milk. He smoothed a ripple from the white cloth before placing a three-tier cake stand at the centre. After two years of rationing, Maudie's stomach groaned at the display:

tiny crustless sandwiches, golden scones accompanied by a thick curl of clotted cream, and two sweet tarts piled with glazed berries.

"Tuck in," said Flower, and Maudie poured tea and closed her eyes to taste the delicate balance of cucumber and horseradish.

"Heavenly," she murmured, tempting him to take a sandwich. He swallowed it whole and blinked.

"Didn't taste a thing," he said, and gobbled two more. "The rest are yours." He pushed the cake stand towards her.

She reached for another sandwich and put it on the rose-patterned tea plate. "I want to hear about your plans to be a musician."

Flower leaned forward, eager. "I've been offered a job with a dance band. A violinist is leaving and the bandleader wants a sax player instead. I'll be playing jazz." His body vibrated as his broad fingers pedalled the padded keys of an imaginary instrument. Maudie could almost hear a syncopated melody.

"What tune are you playing?"

"*Characteristic Blues*. It was written by a jazzman from New Orleans."

"Complicated notes," she said, following his fingers.

Maudie moved onto the scones, splitting one open and spreading it with cream and whole strawberry jam. When Flower's hands came to rest she offered him a filled scone, and he ate it slowly.

"Sidney Bechet played it for the Prince of Wales," he said between mouthfuls.

Maudie nodded. "I've heard he likes jazz."

"*Have* you?"

She beamed at his surprise. "My father made the suit he wore for the jazz concert at Buckingham Palace." Of course, she thought, he doesn't know a thing about me except that I'm a war widow, and an urge to impress overtook her. "The Prince is a fashion enthusiast too, you know." Maudie licked a jammy finger and dabbed her mouth with a napkin. She was eating too much but it anchored her. She drank tea, watching Flower over the slender rim of her cup, appreciating the symmetry of the big handsome head framing the irregular smile.

She saw his mouth tighten as she reached for the top tier of the cake stand. Did he think she was being a glutton? She contemplated the richly-packed fruit tart in her hand. Once she'd eaten it there'd be no more distractions; she'd ask about Harry – was Flower thinking that? She noticed him pat the pocket of his jacket as she bit into an explosion of ripe berries.

They sat in silence while their waiter cleared away empty plates and swept crumbs from the cloth into a little silver dustpan. He left them with a fresh pot of tea, and after a long pause, Flower took a notebook from his pocket and passed it to Maudie.

"Private *David* Hooker's journal," he said. "It was found among your husband's belongings."

Her finger joints stiffened as she reached for it. Her mind was backtracking: Flower had been alert to the bulge of a soldier's notebook while she was devouring pastry. Maudie held it in her lap, smoothing the canvas-bound cover, tracing the band of baggy elastic holding it closed.

"David had something to do with it, didn't he?" Her voice was hoarse.

"I haven't read the journal, but yes, there is a connection." Flower massaged numbness from his left thigh. "It's the reason I wanted to come in person; to give you the background, put Harry's court martial into context."

"What took you so long?"

Flower choked on a mouthful of tea, but there was no rancour in her tone.

"It's a fair question," he said, mopping his tie. "The chaplain died in the field before he could send it to the family, and when it was passed to me there was no forwarding address." He drained his cup. "I intended bringing it with me on my next home leave, but – there was always another battle."

"Were you injured in the same battle as…?"

Flower glanced at his leg. "I lost it on the Somme, but not till the August of 1918. I was with Harry and David all through the assault on Mametz Wood in 1916."

Maudie sat white-faced and composed. "Tell me everything you know."

Flower shifted in his seat. "Did you know that Harry had been in hospital with shell shock after Loos?"

"He went blind for a bit. He was going to be sent home on leave but he said he couldn't abandon David on the Somme to fight without him – do you think he had a premonition?"

Flower shook his head. "I can't say. All I know is he rejoined us and launched himself into all the preparations for a major assault, and the brigade benefited from his infectious gusto." He cleared his throat and drank more tea. Maudie thought he must be sifting difficult memories. As a neurotic reader of war poets, she didn't find it hard to picture him back on the Somme in the heavy summer rain, with the sodden troops, the trenches filled with sucking mud and the stench of death. But she jumped when he spoke in a military voice.

"Private Harry Hooker was a seasoned frontline man," said Flower. "He and Private David Hooker were fine soldiers who looked out for each other like brothers. This was their last and most exhausting battle; they fought in terrible conditions for a week, leading up to the main target, Mametz Wood."

Maudie's eyes were spectral. "I read about the 'terrible conditions' at Mametz in Siegfried Sassoon's poem – he was there, wasn't he?"

"He was with the Fusiliers. His poetry is devastating – I can't read it." After a long silence he continued.

"On the eighth day, on July 8th, we were caught in a German shell barrage."

Maudie gripped the notebook in her lap.

"Harry and David were in my section of fifteen men. Eight of them were blown to pieces. David was killed by the concussion; there wasn't a mark on his body."

Maudie raised her eyebrows at the detail and Flower said: "It *is* relevant to Harry's story." He paused, and she sensed he was trying to remain detached. "Harry'd been knocked unconscious, and we dragged him back to the trench. The survivors were blinded and choking from all the tear gas. A doctor reported to us after examining David's body in No-Man's Land. He said the impact had shattered the bones of his skull and body, but there wasn't a single external wound.

"When Harry heard this, he became obsessed. He said his cousin's body *had* to be recovered before it was obliterated by more shellfire."

"Obsessed?"

"That was the reason he disobeyed the order to return to battle." Flower breathed heavily. "He did go over the top with the others, but he took a shovel as well as his rifle, and he stopped when he reached David's body. It was still unblemished." Flower sighed. "He'd have known that the stretcher-bearers collected wounded soldiers first; there were thousands that day." He slumped in his seat. "The others went on and Harry started digging a grave. He didn't make much impact in the mud. That's probably when he retrieved the journal from David's pocket."

Their eyes were drawn to the buff-coloured notebook Maudie had laid on the table. She fingered her rigid neck muscles before speaking.

"Did he manage to bury David?"

"He used the shell crater – slid the body into the hole and covered it with soil."

She looked straight at him. "Was he able to catch up with his comrades?"

"He would have done, but he was arrested. He was marking the spot; pushing the barrel of David's rifle into the earth. His name was on the butt."

Maudie gave a hollow laugh. "Buried in a soldier's grave where he fell," she quoted. "So that was my Harry's doing."

Flower waited for more.

"The condolence letter from the army," she said. "That's the phrase they used when they wrote to David's father." She covered her face with her hands and rocked in her chair.

Flower looked at his watch. They'd been there for two hours and he hadn't even begun to tell her about the court-martial and his unvoiced objections. While Maudie was in the Ladies, the hotel's six o'clock shift arrived and started preparing empty tables for an evening event. He listened to ripples of light music drifting through from the foyer and guessed it was Peter the pianist limbering up on the polished grand. He lifted the bluebells from a fluted vase on the table and gave them to Maudie when she returned. He noticed she'd pinched some colour back into her cheeks.

"What would you like to do?" he said. "We could go somewhere else."

"I'd like to go home," said Maudie. "I feel *so* tired. Do you mind?"

"I'm relieved." A huge yawn erupted before he could stifle it. "That's so rude!" Flower clapped a hand over his mouth, but Maudie was smiling. Her empathy and resilience were so palpable that he badly wanted to crush her in his arms; he helped her on with her coat instead.

"Shall we meet again next week when I come to town?"

Maudie picked up the notebook and held the bluebells to her nose. "Yes, please. Thank you for being scrupulous."

A waiter slid over with the bill and Flower searched his pockets and counted out six shillings. As he took the receipt he realised he was alone. Maudie had gone. He wasn't sure if he was insulted that she'd simply buggered off, or impressed by her unequivocal behaviour.

On his way through the foyer he stopped by the grand piano. Peter was playing *Magic in the Air* to himself, an absorbed and transforming expression on his scarred features. Flower walked to the entrance, both legs suddenly moving with a swing, and exchanged smiles with the doorman in his outsized bowler hat.

As the crisp April air fanned his face, Flower jammed on a trilby and pushed both hands into his pockets. He set off through Covent Garden to a new jazz nightspot in Frith Street, composing a blues song as he navigated through theatre crowds. Its ironic title, he decided, would be *I'm A Scrupulous Man*; if anyone else but Maudie had called him that, he'd have headed straight for Poppy's boudoir.

Chapter Ten

An inexplicable weight lodged in her legs as Maudie climbed the stairs. She knew Ace and Annie would bombard her with questions, but her instinct was to crawl under a quilt and disengage. She pushed opened the door, nostrils alert to a brisket stew bubbling on the range, and stood unseen for a moment observing the domestic scene. Annie was kneeling by the coal fire drying her hair, fingering macassar oil through damp strands while Ace stood over her, massaging her scalp till she yelped.

"Too stimulating," whispered Maudie from the doorway.

Ace sprang towards her, flexing bony fingers. "Stimulating's good, isn't it?"

Maudie laid her things on a chair and lunged for her son, tickling the backs of his knees till he slipped to the floor shrieking. He scrubbed his bare legs over the cool wood.

"That was TOO stimulating." His mouth twitched between torment and triumph.

Annie stood up, hair glistening, and stared at the notebook and wilting flowers on the chair by the door.

"Bluebells from the Waldorf tearoom," said Maudie. "They need water, Ace. Shall we put them in that green vase of Bubbe's?"

Ace scrabbled to his feet and went through to the kitchen to find the delicate flute. Its base was a solid glass globe; when he held it up to the light he saw a mysterious world of suspended bubbles. Maudie knew it reminded him of the fizzy explosion he got up his nose when he drank the Tavern's ginger pop: effer-effer-. He'd be trying to remember the word, and she might just have time to prepare Annie before Ace filled the vase with water and rushed back to the living room.

"What's the name..." he began, and she saw him turn to Annie in time to follow the path of a tear down her pale cheek onto the notebook in her hands.

"What is it?" His voice was shrill; he wasn't going to be left out. "Is it from the Flower Soldier?"

Maudie took the slopping vase from his grip. "Help me arrange them," she said.

Ace grabbed the bluebells and stuffed them into the flute. He sniffed and pinched his nose. "They *smell.*"

"They do," agreed Maudie. "It's a scent that reminds me of the woodlands in Kent. Do you remember all the blue flowers? We thought they looked like a carpet."

Ace opened his eyes wide, and then it came to him.

"Effer-vescent," he said, before a sob from Annie reminded him of something else.

"Where does that book *come* from?"

"It *is* from the Flower Soldier," said Maudie. He gave it to me for Annie's family; it belonged to her brother."

"Did he write in it? Did he write about my father?" Ace stood in front of Annie, eyes on the notebook.

Maudie sat him down beside her, wondering how she could give him the proof he craved. Perhaps there would be something in David's journal.

"John Flower told me today that your father was a very brave soldier."

Ace watched her face.

"He was knocked unconscious by shellfire, but as soon as he recovered he climbed out of the trench to save Annie's brother."

"Where was he?"

"Lying in the field – the battlefield. He'd been hit."

Ace leapt to his feet, hair on end. "Was he bleeding a lot?"

"No." Maudie glanced at Annie, who was chaotically stirring the stew. "He was dead."

Ace sat down again with a bump and Maudie sighed. How could she explain this to a little boy when she hardly understood it herself.

"You can't save someone who's already dead." His voice was accusing.

"Your father made him a grave with his name so he'd never be called an unknown soldier; so we'd always know where he was buried."

This was news to Annie. She dropped her spoon in the pot and reached out to press her friend's hand. A random piece of cooked carrot remained in Maudie's palm; she couldn't have explained how a bit of vegetable spoke of intimacy, but she gazed at the talisman for some moments before flicking it into the hearth. The supper pot rumbled on the range, the fire sizzled and St Anne's clock chimed the hour. As the seventh bell faded, Ace moved closer to his mother.

"Is my father an unknown soldier?"

Maudie gathered him into her arms. "Oh no, my darling. When I meet John Flower next week he'll tell me where we can find your father's grave in France. We'll go there oneday; we'll plant bluebells."

Tucking Ace into bed that night, she noticed he had Mr B the Bear squashed up beside him – a habit he'd dropped when he started school. Maudie crouched on the rug by the bed, smoothing the bristled tufts of her son's hair, trying to recall herself at the age of six. Yes, the comfort of a mute bear with lugubrious eyes would have been preferable to an overwrought parent fumbling with words to explain loss. She touched her head to his, and crept away to discuss inadequacy with Annie.

Annie was back in the workroom preparing materials for the morning; they had Chelsea Flower Show orders to clear before starting on the summer hats for Derby Day. First she polished the iron matrice they used for shaping the brims of stiff hats, and made small adjustments to the wooden flanging frame for widening soft brims. Then she gathered together all the stray pieces of jade green felt, and sorted methodically through plaits of straw and petersham ribbon. And through all the preparations, tears splashed unchecked over everything until she started laughing and hugging herself.

"I'm not mad," she said when Maudie came into the room. "Well, a little. I never expected anything of David's from the war." She blew her nose and sniffed. "I know it really belongs to my father and I'll give it to him soon, but holding this notebook makes me feel near him."

Maudie sat on her work chair. "You're so positive Annie. So – uncluttered."

"Simple, you mean. But not so simple that I haven't detected *your* undercurrents."

Maudie opened her mouth to protest, but Annie spread her hands. "Please, I know it's been horrifying to stir up the grief; to go back to all that bleakness. But isn't there a lighter side?"

Maudie shrugged. "The tea was a wonderful treat."

"What about John Flower, otherwise known as the Flower Soldier?"

"What about him?" She tried to sound neutral.

"Listen, something tells me that even with freshly-oiled hair I won't stand a chance now he's met you."

Maudie gave in. Only Annie could winkle out the truth. She confessed to heart flutters under Annie's scrutiny, and made her friend gasp when she described the encounter in Walkers Court a week earlier.

"He staggered into you because he's got an artificial leg? When did he lose it?"

"A few weeks before the war ended." Maudie paused. "Isn't that ironic – he'd already done four years of active service without a scratch."

"Well," said Annie, "the Greek Street baker's son was killed on the last *day* of the war.

"Of course." Maudie's voice dropped to a whisper.

"The hopping Flower lives!" Annie seemed determined to maintain a celebratory tone to the evening.

"He does *not* hop." She caught the impudent grin on Annie's face and wagged a finger at her. "You…how can a minx like you be my friend?"

"It's a shallow friendship, isn't it?" Annie pulled Maudie from her chair and danced her round the room. She stopped suddenly.

"John Flower probably can't dance."

Maudie stood on one leg, considering. "It might be a problem, but he can play the music and you and I will dance."

Annie tangoed over to a cupboard and took out a bottle of brandy and two glasses. She poured generous measures and handed one to Maudie. "Here's to shallow friendship."

They sat side by side, toasting their bare feet in front of the embers, and Maudie caught herself noticing that this was happiness, before her thoughts slid back to Ace.

"Will you read David's notebook before you give it to Aaron?"

Annie lifted her head from Maudie's shoulder. "I'm tempted to, but he should be the one to read it first." She swallowed the rest of her brandy. "David's handwriting was always dreadful; it would take me ages to decipher, and every day I'd feel guilty of depriving Father. Better he shares it with us, don't you think?"

Maudie nodded, but her skin contracted thinking of Ace in bed with his bear. She sensed a potential source of backup drifting away from her; the reconstruction of an authentic hero-father was so much more complicated than she'd imagined. Her throat filled as a thought occurred: maybe Ace's loss was greater than her own.

Chapter Eleven

August 1926

Ace watched John Flower distorting his mouth into a silent snarl. In quick succession, he leered, bared his teeth, exposed his gums, and puckered his stretched lips.

"Why the hideous faces?"

"I'm exercising muscles." Flower smacked himself in the face. "They need to be flexible before I play."

His one-room flat off Charing Cross Road was above a musical instrument shop, where no-one was ever disturbed by his playing. Ace sat on the shabby chaise-longue beside a table heaped with sheet music, taking in the tousled bed, the pipe ash on the carpet, his host's unshaven chin. He wondered if Flower was disturbed by his random visit.

The day before, Maudie had taken him to a performance at the Savoy Hotel, and for the first time in his life the neurotic spasms of his twelve-year-old body had made sense. The jitters in his legs matched the jazz rhythms of the band, and the muscular sounds Flower produced on his alto saxophone touched places Ace knew only in his dreams. He *had* to be a musician.

As usual on a Sunday, he'd spent the morning with his grandfather, helping him stitch a broad-shouldered suit for the proprietor of the *Illustrated London News*. Zeidy was training him in all aspects of tailoring, expecting Ace to take over the family business one day before he was crippled by the arthritis creeping into his finger joints. Ace tried to be attentive, but he much preferred running errands or hefting the steam iron.

Here in Flower's tobacco-stained lair, he glimpsed a job he could be passionate about. The coarse fibres of the chair poked and scratched at his legs, but he sat perfectly still while Flower mobilised his mouth. When he was handed the instrument case, Ace laid it beside him, knowing a soppy grin was stretching his cheeks.

"Open it," said Flower. Ace raised the lid and lifted out the gleaming brass sax. "Now find a curved tube; yes, that's the crook and you slide it into the neck."

Ace followed instructions, attaching a reed to the mouthpiece, which he then fitted onto the crook. Flower inspected the instrument before putting the sling round his neck.

He lifted pale eyebrows. "You've done a good job," he said, sliding the mouthpiece up and down. He blew long notes through the sax. Ace hugged his knees as he looked at Flower standing tall with his legs apart; it seemed not to matter that one leg was false.

"I'm going to play scales till I get them running. Might take a while. Are you thirsty?" Ace shook his head. He later learned he was listening to Flower's regular practice: up the sharps and down the flats in a cycle of fifths, followed by arpeggios played in rapid ascending progression, four notes in each chord. But that Sunday afternoon he simply absorbed waves of sound that had him leaping about, and when it was time to go home, he walked with a purposeful tread down the undulating stairs, fitting his feet into shoe-shaped hollows.

"Tell your ma I'll be along soon," Flower called down, and Ace remembered this was the day he came to Meard Street for his weekly bath.

"I want to learn the sax," Ace said to Maudie, but the street doorbell jangled before she could reply. He raised the window and leaned out to see Flower looking up, clear-eyed and clean-shaven beneath a jaunty boater. He bundled the key into a sock and lobbed it out of the window. They'd never needed to lock the communal street door before, but someone had taken to using the hallway as a urinal, and the coal stock in the back yard was diminishing.

Flower appeared, dropping the key and a bag on the table before kissing Maudie. Ace already guessed what was in the bag; his focus was on the nature of Flower's kiss – was it dry and friendly, or sloppy and romantic? Over the years he and Pierre had speculated on Flower's relationship with Maudie. At first they thought he was going to marry Annie; she was the one who made him laugh and persuaded him onto the dance-floor. With Maudie he was dark and twitchy, like Zeidy's melancholy pedlar, while she simply vanished behind her doughy currant-bun look.

"Don't you even like him?" Ace had asked her after Flower clumped off down the stairs one heavy winter afternoon. Maudie looked up from the hat she was finishing and stared at him.

"Why 'even'? I do like him, very much."

"What I mean is, you look miserable when he's here." Ace imitated her grim expression, and Maudie went to the mirror to see for herself.

"I look awful! I'm getting gloomy creases." She smoothed her cheeks upwards with her palms. "Talking about your father with him confuses me..." Her voice tailed away and Ace fiddled with feather trimmings on the worktable.

"Pierre says you prob'ly feel disloyal thinking about another man."

"Ace! Do you two discuss my private life?"

"Course we do!" Ace had thrown the feathers in the air and run laughing from the room.

Now, six years later, as he watched them kiss, he made loud gagging noises.

"That's enough namby-pamby," he said, forcing himself between them.

Flower put his arm round Ace. "I was going to have a bath before I asked your mother a rather important question, but perhaps this is the moment." A flush was seeping into his blond eyebrows.

"Maudie, I've been invited to New Orleans. I've been asked to play with jazzmen there." Flower studied the backs of his hands. "I want you to sail to America with me – for a holiday."

"A holiday!"

"Can I come too?" Ace thought it was worth a try, but no-one was listening to him. Flower was holding Maudie's hands and mumbling.

"You know what I'm trying to say: I'm asking you to marry me. The cruise will be our honeymoon."

"I will, I will. Yes, *please*." Maudie lifted his hands to her face and kissed his fingertips. Their tenderness with each other reminded Ace of Mama and Papa Pierre together.

"I'll stay with Pierre while you're away," he said in the deepest voice he could muster.

Maudie looked from Flower to her son. " You two have been plotting this together!"

Ace said nothing, but he leaned against Flower, experiencing a sensation he'd never had before.

★★★

"Don't look down." Pierre was shouting from the opposite bank. "Look at me and walk."

They'd all been down at the river, where part of an obstacle course was to cross the wide water on a narrow bridge of twisted tree trunks. The flow was fast after a night of rain. As Ace looked down a whirling in his head caused his legs to seize. He tried to shuffle forward but his feet were rooted.

Ace glanced at his friend on the other side, prancing about in plimsolls. Boys behind Ace were waiting to cross. "Get a move on," said one, shoving him in the back.

Something inside him gave way. He tottered backwards, spun round and pushed through the jostling boys. The dizziness passed as he ran from their jeering. What was the matter with him? Why did he have to hide? In the tent he shared with Pierre, he pulled on the Fair Isle jumper Bubbe had knitted, feeling frozen. It was the middle of summer and the sun was hot, but camping with the school in Kent had challenged his resources.

Pierre always had a theory. "That was vertigo," he said, while Ace sniffed his clammy skin, convinced he could smell fear. He grabbed a pillow and thumped it repeatedly against his head before speaking.

"Do you think cowardice can be inherited?"

Pierre flopped on his canvas bed, flicking curled duck feathers off the blanket. "Don't be daft, Ace. Didn't the Flower Soldier tell you your father was a brave man?"

"He never explained properly. What's brave about burying your dead cousin while your fellow soldiers are risking their lives fighting the enemy?" He picked a clod of earth off his shoe and hurled it through the tent flap.

"Ask him to explain properly."

Ace shook his head. "He won't talk about the war anymore. He says the nightmares come back when he starts remembering."

Pierre flung his muddy shoes into a corner. "Well, I don't think cowardice is hereditary. Why don't you ask your mother?"

"Because I know what she'll say. You'd think my father was the most wonderful human being ever, listening to her. She says to me, *you're just like him*."

"You don't know how lucky you are, do you? I heard that Stuttering Henry's mother can't stand him because he's careless like his father was. She blames the father for getting killed and leaving her to bring up the brat on her own."

"Did she actually say 'brat'?"

"Well, that's what Henry told me."

Ace thought about this, but it didn't make him feel lucky. Of course his mother adored him. Whatever happened, he sensed he could depend on her belief in him. But what about the rest of the world?

Chapter Twelve

September 1926

Maudie stood at the window framed by red-gold leaves. Her gaze shifted from the fringe of autumn to the watchmaker who lived opposite; he was peering through his magnifying glass at what she imagined to be a ruby. It was only eight o'clock. She stretched and sighed, aware of space. The millinery season was over for the year and Ace wasn't due back from school camp until early afternoon. The morning was hers. She had one late summer order from a regular client and then she could start on her travelling trousseau. As the thought registered, her stomach convulsed and she clamped her arms round her waist.

" You've got the curse?" Annie came into the workroom with an armful of fabric.

Maudie relaxed her grip. " I think that was a touch of wedding jitters."

"You're not having regrets!" Annie's voice was sharp as she dropped her load on the table.

"Oh, no. John's the man for me." She moved to the other end of the table and started sifting through sisal plaits. "But I think I've just realised how different it'll be. I'm thirty-five, Annie, and I'm so used to being independent."

Annie swivelled the gold band on her left hand. "I've adjusted, haven't I?"

We both did, thought Maudie, remembering her anxiety over Annie's lightning romance with mercurial Albie, the Scottish photographer who worked for *Vogue*. When they married, Annie moved out of the windowless room at Meard Street and Maudie had briefly panicked. But here they were three years later, still working together, still close friends.

"You're much younger than me," said Maudie. She began weaving the straw plaits in a circular shape from the crown to the edge of the brim.

"I'm only eight years younger, you know; sharp enough to keep the business going while you're gallivanting abroad with your beau."

"He'll be my husband by then," said Maudie, "and I'll be Mrs Flower!"

"About time too." Annie began flicking through the pages of a new *Vanity Fair*. "All those wasted years tormenting each other with the past. I suppose it was an important process…"

"It was, because now it *is* the past; it's not lingering about in the shadows." Maudie looked up from back-weaving the hat. "I didn't even know about the first Mrs Flower till recently."

Annie stopped leafing through the magazine. "What happened to her? He wouldn't tell *me*."

"She died in childbirth."

"Oh, how awful. What about the baby?"

"He died too."

Annie leaned back in her chair and groaned. "I had no idea. I was so flippant with him, so teasing about his mysterious wife. When did it happen?"

"The winter of 1915." Maudie cupped the hat between her hands. "John was on home leave. He had them buried together and went straight back to France." She picked up a stray length of thread and wound it tightly round a finger. "He said the slaughter on the battlefield was more comprehensible. He never took home leave again."

Annie rose from the chair, face stiff and white as calico. "I'll fill the kettle," she said, but went over to Maudie and stood beside her. Maudie put an arm round her narrow waist.

"No shadows, remember? It's part of the past." She pushed Annie gently towards the door and unravelled the thread from her finger.

By the time Annie came back from the kitchen with a tray of tea and buttered buns, Maudie was pressing the hat into shape on a wooden block. They sat side by side eating breakfast, and after pouring a second cup Annie sat back with a sigh.

"Do you ever wonder about what's in David's notebook?"

Maudie paused for a moment, wiping her work-snagged fingers carefully on a napkin. "No," she said, "not anymore. I used to imagine it would explain everything, but Uncle Aaron didn't think so, did he?"

"No, but it's odd how Father kept it to himself." Annie swallowed tea in a hunched position and coughed. "I used to ask him to lend it to us, but he wouldn't be parted from it." She put her cup on the tray. "I wish I'd read it first."

"I wish you had, too." Maudie fingered up a breadcrumb from the table and popped it in her mouth. "Now listen, let's get back to the present. I need your help on a pressing matter."

Annie snapped to attention, brushing her forehead with the back of a hand. Maudie wanted her to choose the sort of clothes she should take on her honeymoon. She took down the latest copy of *Vogue* from the shelf of fashion magazines and skimmed the pages until she came to the designs of Coco Chanel.

"Look at that!" Annie's finger stabbed at the silhouette of a simple knee-length frock. "That's so elegant; we'll make you one of those in black for a start."

Maudie stared at the picture. "It's a bit short for me."

"Nonsense. You've got good legs, and that length is the height of fashion."

"For flappers, maybe." Maudie pulled up her calf-length skirt and surveyed her legs.

" Just like a showgirl's!"

"Get away with you." Maudie shook out her skirt. "I suppose that length's possible, but I won't be rolling down my stockings and powdering my knees."

Annie rolled her eyes. "No, you certainly will not. This is a classic style – you're going to look the *bee's* knees." Thinking aloud she murmured, "You'll need one beautiful floaty evening gown and lots of pretty underwear." She turned to pages of lingerie and read out a piece about the drastic decline of corset sales.

"What a relief they've gone out of fashion," said Maudie, and then clapped a hand to the side of her head. "But isn't one of your sisters a corset-maker?"

"She was, but Mildred's adaptable. Now she makes camisoles and petticoats." Annie was bending over the magazine. "She could make you one of these elastic girdles to hold up your stockings and, look at these, you must have cami-knickers – silk ones, don't you think?"

Maudie scrutinised the illustrations. "Irresistible," she said, "*and* they look comfortable."

"You'll be shimmying the night away in them," said Annie, and suddenly sat very still.

"What is it?"

Annie hesitated. "I know it's none of my business, but I just wondered: is John physically capable of being your husband?"

Maudie's wide speckled eyes answered Annie's question.

"Sorry to probe." Annie covered her face with her hands, but Maudie caught the shine of her eyes through finger spaces.

"You're priceless, Annie, and I love you for being curious. I was anxious myself, but John's an inventive man and, yes, he's *very* physically capable..."

Annie jumped up. "You devil! You know already! Good for you." She sat down again and drummed her feet on the floor.

"It happened –" Maudie was saying, when her voice was obliterated by elephants thundering up the stairs. The workroom door burst open and there stood two suntanned boys with a whiff of wild beast about them.

"We're back," said Ace, and simultaneously he and Pierre dropped their canvas packs to the floor and stepped forward to give the women rough hugs.

Maudie caught her breath, thinking how beautiful they were. Their golden faces shone, their shoulders looked muscled and they seemed so – manly.

"When did you two last have a wash?" She pulled a bit of twig from Ace's stiff hair.

"The day we left," said Pierre. He scratched his head with both hands, and they all looked down at the debris falling from his hair.

"We have been camping, you know," said Ace, "and water conservation *is* important."

"Subtle point," said Maudie. She noticed that the familial slope of his eyes would soon be seductive.

"I want to know if you learned to cook," said Annie, initiating a catalogue of campfire disaster stories from the boys while they raked through their packs for the black toffees they'd made.

Ace sniggered. "We acquired a taste for burnt food, but Pierre's herb potato cakes were the best; he served them with edible flowers. Mr Fiber said his cooking was sophisticated."

Pierre picked up a white napkin left on the table from breakfast and tied it round his head. "I'm going to be a chef," he swaggered.

Ace cast around for something appropriate and found only a toasting fork. With legs apart, he pursed his lips to the handle and pedalled his fingers against the brass stem.

"A sax player!" said Pierre. "Ace is going to be a jazz musician like the Flower Soldier."

Ace jousted the tines of the fork at Pierre, who pulled off his chef's hat and parried with the napkin, whipping the fork from Ace's hand and sending it spinning across the floor.

"Enough!" said Maudie, as they wrestled each other to the floor. "Respect for the workroom, please." They lay panting on a crumpled rug, still boys after all. Maudie glanced at Annie who was spitting out a toffee.

"Ugh, my tongue's shrunk!"

"That'll be the treacle," said Pierre, sitting up. "It's a vital ingredient."

"Well, I have to tell you this is the nastiest sweet I've ever tasted." Annie wrapped the sticky lump in a scrap of newspaper and dropped it in the bin.

Ace leapt to his feet. "My friend and I are *deeply* offended. I don't know how we're going to forgive you."

"The only way," said Pierre, "is if she makes us apple turnovers. What d'you think, Ace?"

Ace nodded and slung an arm round Pierre. Their heads touched – one dark, one fair – and Maudie saw they had a balanced friendship of equal dependence. Her fatherless son had cruised smoothly into adolescence, and she could sail away with John for six weeks without him missing her.

Her eyelids prickled. Maudie had a sensation that although she was the one going away, it was Ace who would actually take wing.

Chapter Thirteen

There was a wildness in him that day as he stood on the docks at Southampton. The wind matched his mood, snatching loutishly at his open jacket. He wrestled to fasten it, and watched a button spin away, trailing broken thread.

Ace turned to Pierre and flipped him behind the knees with a bony ankle, bringing him to the ground with a cry. Their game of dead-leg, usually good-natured, took on an edge of menace; they kicked at each other until both were numb. Only then did Ace take in the scale of the cliff-sized ship with four funnels that loomed in the rackety harbour. And there were the passengers, Maudie and Flower, leaning against each other on the quayside. He'd insisted on seeing the boat that would take the newlyweds to America, and Aaron was chaperoning the boys, stirred, he said, by memories of his voyage to London thirty-five years before.

"What's the name of it? Aaron squinted at the ship. "My old eyes can't read it."

Ace spelled it out: "A-Q-U-I-T-A-N-I-A. I don't know how to say it. What does it mean?"

"Aquitania – how should I know? Something auspicious, I'm sure." It seemed an inadequate answer to Ace, but he filed away another new word.

He wanted to see everything, but crew members were already bellowing 'All ashore' to visitors, and only passengers were allowed up the gangway. He had to make do with Maudie pointing out the porthole that might be the window of their second-class cabin. Aaron approached one of the greasers smoking a Woodbine on the dock, and learned about the modern turbine steam engines powering the liner.

Ace studied his mother. She was wearing her new black wool coat with its shawl collar of chinchilla fur. The cherry lining echoed her frock, and her lipstick matched as well. Shingled hair curled from under a cloche pinned with a scarab-gem brooch, and in her ankle-strap shoes with two-inch heels she just reached Flower's shoulder. Ace watched his new stepfather adjusting his mole-brown trilby and tweaking the left trouser leg of the tweed suit tailored by Maudie's father; who did they remind him of? He remembered a stage show he'd seen of a dancing couple – that was it, they had the glamour of Fred Astaire and his sister.

Embarkation and sailing time approached; the group drew together while a sweaty tension developed in the urgent shouts of ship workers and crew operating to a deadline. As the commotion swelled, Ace shrank inside himself. His mother was going away. Then she was beside him, lifting his hand, pressing something into the palm and closing his fingers over it.

"By the time you've solved it, I'll be home," she said.

Maudie blew a kiss from the gangway, and Ace felt it land like a breeze on his face before Aaron led them away to catch their train back to London.

In the carriage Ace drew out of his pocket the envelope that had been folded into a palm-sized square by his mother.

"What is it?" Pierre leaned over, inquisitive fingers smoothing the paper.

"*Wait.*" Ace shielded the envelope from view. "I've got to look first." Moments later he was nudging his friend. "It's a treasure hunt! She says they'll be home before we've worked out all the clues."

"Ha! We'll show her."

"Listen to this," said Ace. " 'I'm used to beat precious metal thin as a leaf. You'll find me held high in a Soho street.' Then the next line says: 'When you're standing in sight of me, read the next clue.' "

"What *is* the next clue?" Pierre rocked in his seat as the train speeded up.

"It's a direction, leading us to another clue I suppose. But wait, we don't know what the first one is, do we?"

They both looked blank and turned to Aaron, sitting opposite with his newspaper.

"Something to do with gold?" His finger was on a news item.

Ace gazed at fields rolling by. "Gold-leaf! I've heard of that. What's it beaten with – a hammer?"

Aaron looked up. "Probably, but we don't have any gold-beaters in the family to ask."

"So, we have to find a hammer hanging in the street." Pierre rapped his head with his knuckles. "Ha, maybe a *picture* of one on a tavern sign. Is there a Gold-beaters Arms?"

"Your father would know." Aaron was still reading.

The train whistle echoed through the night and Ace peered through smut-streaked windows for familiar landmarks; there was treasure in the streets of London.

By the time they reached Waterloo Station both boys were asleep. Aaron went to find his pony and trap while Ace and Pierre stood shaky and disorientated on the platform.

"You two look shipwrecked," said the driver as they hauled themselves into the trap. Ace recognised the voice: Aaron's daughter Mildred was holding the reins. He tried to think of a cheeky remark about the cami-knickers she'd made for his mother, but 'somnolent' was the only word he uttered as his body folded into a tartan rug beside his comatose friend.

He woke next morning in the flat above the Dean Street Tavern.

"Petit dejeuner, young man," said Mama Pierre, and Ace bounced out of bed for the hot croissants and bowls of coffee she served. Pierre was already sitting at the kitchen table, mouth jammed with pastry.

"I've asked Papa." His voice was indistinct and flakes of breakfast sprayed from his lips. He apologised to his mother and started again. "My papa says there's no gold-beaters public-house in Soho, but he thinks your grandfather Zeidy will know someone in the trade."

Ace looked up from dunking a croissant. "He does know a lot of people." He jerked upright. "It's Sunday, isn't it?"

Pierre nodded and Ace flexed his fingers. "I have to go and be his apprentice this morning. Well, I'll ask him about gold hammers."

"And if he knows where to find one in the street you *have* to come and get me first." Pierre fixed him with a glint.

Zeidy was not only familiar with gold craftsmen, he knew they had a guild with headquarters in Soho.

"Smaller stitches," he instructed, as Ace tacked the collar and lapels to a tweed jacket. "A mallet is the tool they use. I don't remember seeing one on public display, but I wonder..."

Ace stopped working. "What?"

"Keep basting while I talk. I do remember a discussion about the craft's symbol – the mallet. Members wanted a gold one mounted on the building."

"Where's the building?" Ace squawked as he pushed the needle into his finger.

Zeidy sighed, his own arthritic fingers labouring along the turn-ups of the trousers he was finishing. "Concentration is important. There will always be distractions, but you will learn to be focused." He contemplated Ace's erratic stitches and patted his pricked hand. "It may take some time."

Ace knew with certainty he could never satisfy his grandfather's tailoring standards.

"You're a wise man Zeidy, and I'll try to learn from you – but *please* tell me where this building is."

"Tell me first why you're so interested in the gold-beaters."

Aware of his grandfather's indifference to Maudie, Ace charmed him with the tale of a school educational quiz, sewing diligently as he talked.

His grandfather beamed. "So easy from here. Walk through the square, come out at Greek Street and turn left. It's near the *shul* in Manette Street."

Ace bent to his work, attempting to keep the stitches even, forcing himself to concentrate on the subtle colouring of the rough wool. He felt disloyal to Maudie for his small deceit and found himself blurting out the truth, not looking at Zeidy but hearing a brisk intake of breath. When he did look, the reproach in his grandfather's lined face only spurred Ace to reveal another unwelcome truth.

"I want to be a musician." In the silence that followed, he added: "I think it would suit me better."

"You think it would suit you better." Zeidy repeated the words like a judgement. "I fear for you." His cold eyes were difficult to look at, and Ace imagined icy fingers creeping along his spine as Zeidy leaned towards him.

"Your mother spirited Harry away from me, and now she's married another man who is spiriting *you* away from me."

Ace screwed up his face, trying to grasp at logic while his grandfather took the work from his hands.

"You may as well go now; I'm wasting my time with you. Go waste your time looking for treasure."

A man Ace loved had dismissed him. He couldn't think of anything to say. How could Zeidy do that to him, scour him of words? When his grandfather showed him to the door, he simply floated out in a daze before speeding away to collect Pierre.

It was lunchtime, and Papa Pierre blocked their escape till the rush was over. While Pierre was serving food to customers, Ace was sent into the kitchen, where Mama Pierre ladled out a bowl of thick bean soup and sat him down with a chunk of crusty bread and a glass of diluted wine.

"It's all very fine for you!" Pierre flung himself onto a kitchen chair and glared at Ace, rosy-cheeked and dimpled after his fortifying lunch.

"Listen, I'd have gone by myself, but I waited for you."

"I know, I know. I'm tired." Pierre let his head hang forward and gave out a ragged sigh.

"And you're hungry." His mother slid a bowl of soup in front of him. "Eat first, then go looking for your golden hamlet."

She had no idea why they gagged with laughter, but the word slipped effortlessly into their shared vocabulary. When they finally stood at the western end of Manette Street looking up at a muscular arm grasping the tool of the gold-beaters' trade, they chanted in unison: "The golden hamlet!"

"First clue solved in one day," said Pierre. "Thanks to your Zeidy."

"He's not *my* Zeidy – he's a bitter old man."

Pierre glanced at his friend's forlorn face. "Did you ruin a suit?"

"I ruined everything. I told him I wanted to be a musician."

"Let him stew for a bit," said Pierre. "You don't want to be a tailor anyway, do you? It was brave what you told him."

A fragment of light penetrated his gloom and Ace looked at the crumpled sheet he was holding. "Read out the next clue," said Pierre.

Ace consulted the paper. "Number two is simple: 'Ring on the bell in front of you and ask at the desk for a letter addressed to Ace Hooker Esquire.' "

"That's not fair. No-one's going to be at Gold-beaters House on a Sunday."

They rang the bell anyway and slumped against the solid door. "After school tomorrow?" said Ace.

"Have to be, though it's bookbinding with Mr Fiber when classes finish."

Ace thought about this, picking at a splinter of wood on the door. "Well," he said, "I think Mr Fiber would be interested in our treasure hunt, don't you? If we tell him about it he'll prob'ly give us ten minutes to collect the next clue."

Mr Fiber's nose quivered like a bloodhound's when Ace explained what they were up to. "Your mother is a most perceptive lady," he said. "Off you go, but no dawdling. And if there are fiendishly difficult clues along the way, I'll try to help – if I'm allowed."

"Yes please, Sir!" They barged through the school gate and pelted across three streets till they stood under the golden arm. A guild official let them in, bemused by their request until he found the letter in a pigeonhole marked 'H'. Outside, Ace tore open the envelope and together they read:

'My natural home is a mountainous region

I'm here in Soho to guide those

Led by the nose'

"Fiendishly difficult," said Ace, and they ran back to school to involve Mr Fiber.

While he showed the bookbinding group how to make leather-bound covers, the headmaster read out the clue and invited comments.

"I'm th-th-thinking of an animal," said Henry.

"Something to do with perfume," said another pupil.

"Scented flowers."

"A horse and cart."

"What do *you* think Sir?" said Pierre.

Mr Fiber shook his grey curls. "I simply have no idea."

"But Sir," said Ace, "you're the clever one."

"Evidently not clever enough." Mr Fiber tapped a hairy nostril. "But I'll think about it, and when we meet next week to emboss leather, we'll compare ideas."

"A week!" Pierre's eyes blazed. "We can't wait that long."

"Then I expect you'll solve it yourselves and enlighten the rest of us," he said, gathering up an armful of books.

"*Enlighten* them," said Ace, as they scuffed their way home to Pierre's. "Who else can we ask?"

Pierre shrugged. "He's an imbecile."

At the end of school next day Mr Fiber beckoned to Ace in the playground. "I may have solved your clue," he said, "but I need you to verify it."

Ace extracted Pierre from a game of Ping-Pong on the lab table and together they sprinted to Old Compton Street, steaming up the tobacconist's window with their breath.

"We're here to verify Mr Fiber's discovery." Ace wiped the window with his sleeve. "He said to look for something tartan."

They squashed their noses against the glass until Pierre looked sideways at the doorway. "What's that wooden man in a kilt doing there?"

The tobacconist appeared from behind the figure, puffing on a cigar. "Couldn't help overhearing," he said. "Your headmaster was in here yesterday buying tobacco, and he asked about the Highlander. Have you come to collect the letter your mother left with me?"

Ace thought of her planting clues all over town for him, and he fingered his ribcage where it seemed to be squeezing his heart. He patted the tall kilted figure as they followed Mr Krantz into the shop.

"He's very old, from Georgian times, when shopkeepers used him to advertise the availability of snuff." The tobacconist shuffled through papers looking for Ace's envelope. "They stood a

Highlander in the doorway so gentlemen would know they could step inside and refill their snuffboxes." Mr Krantz's voice now came from under the counter. "The king's wife was known as Sniffy Charlotte, y'know."

The boys shuffled about; they were more interested in the glass jars of sweets he sold. And they wanted the next clue.

"We'd like a hap'orth each of tiger nuts and sherbert please," said Ace, to move things along.

The next clue was straightforward and directed them to the organ grinder who played in the street with a parrot. When a penny was dropped in his tin, the parrot jumped into a box of folded paper fortunes and picked one out for the donor. The boys were instructed to offer a penny each in exchange for a sealed envelope from the entertainer.

"Your mother's gone to a lot of trouble to keep us occupied," said Pierre, "but it's days before the organ man comes to Soho – do you ever see him except at weekends?"

"When's the winkle man here? I've heard the organ when I go to buy cockles for Annie."

"Exactly – that's a Sunday." Pierre counted on his fingers. "Five days away!"

"Sunday," repeated Ace. The day I don't go to Zeidy's anymore..."

They looked at each other. "Shall we play chess in your room?" Ace tapped out a rhythm on his cheeks to disguise the wobble in his voice.

"Prob'ly not." Pierre was balancing on kerbstones like a tightrope walker. "If we go home now, Papa will make us work. I've got a better idea. Let's go and see his friend Mr Baird; he's got a funny attic in Frith Street where he's invented something with moving pictures – I want to see it."

Their visit to the engineer and his prototype 'television' solved one of the treasure hunt riddles long before they got to it. Maudie had them tracking clues all over town until, six weeks later, they solved number twenty and took possession of a small silver key.

"Now what happens?" Ace searched Grandfather Lock's benign face for guidance. The trail had led them to the tailoring shop in Savile Row where he handed them the key and Maudie's final envelope. He was leaning comfortably on the counter in his rolled up sleeves and waistcoat, with a tape measure looped around his neck.

"Where's the treasure?" Ace was hopping from one agitated leg to the other. "We *have* to claim it before they get back."

"Better read the letter," said his grandfather.

"How can she do that?" Ace threw down the note. "We have to wait till they get back!"

Pierre picked up the note. 'Just in case you read this before John and I are home – CONGRATULATIONS. Have the key ready to unlock your treasure as soon as we land.'

They wouldn't stay for tea because neither of them could keep still. "Sorry Gramps, but we're ferociously disappointed," said Ace.

His grandfather laid a calming hand on each boy's shoulder. "Delayed gratification has its merits," he said. "You have a whole day before they return to savour the certainty of treasure."

Stomping back towards Pierre's, they passed a rag and bone man offering ornaments in exchange for junk, and for a second Ace was tempted to give him the key. As they turned into Walker's Court, a heavy scent settled over them.

"Lily of the valley?" Ace sniffed as a vision in purple rayon stepped from a doorway.

"If it isn't my handsome Flash Harry!" Poppy's husky voice drew them close enough to be stirred by her kohl-rimmed eyes and the shimmery flare of her short skirt. She lifted Ace's chin with nicotine-stained fingers and frowned. "Are you cross about something, love?"

When he explained about the thwarted treasure hunt, Poppy swayed her hips.

"You can hunt for *my* treasure anytime you like." She pinched his cheek and laughed herself into a coughing fit. Pierre thumped her on the back until she begged him to stop.

"Monsewer, you've saved me life." She was gasping as she handed him a cigarette with a box of matches. "Light it for me, will you, petit choux, while I get me breath back."

The blind violinist began playing at the end of the street and Poppy swore.

"I won't be able to bear much of that – it always makes me cry."

Ace remembered her tears the first day he met her. "Why were you crying then?" he said.

Poppy hesitated. "Ask me when your voice breaks. Now, you tell me about your mother: what's she doing going on a ship to America? Very lah-di-dah."

"Lah-di-dah." Ace giggled. "She married John Flower and they're on their honeymoon."

Poppy twirled in her skirt. "Well, well," she said with an expression on her face that Ace couldn't interpret. "The Flower Soldier, eh? Your mother's a lucky lady, I can tell you."

Chapter Fourteen

1932

Emerging from the dense heat of a nightclub in Charing Cross Road, Ace slicked back a thick crest of hair with the sweat of his palms. He noticed his hands were still vibrating. The Original Dixieland Jazz Band from New Orleans were in town, thrilling audiences wherever they played, and with John Flower as his mentor, Ace was going to all their shows.

Maudie's silver key had opened an instrument case, and inside he'd found a saxophone on jade velvet. His fidgety body wrapped itself around the brass; he fingered the padded keys operated by a complicated system of rods and levers, and blew through the mouthpiece with a force that surprised him. He'd been right: he *was* more suited to playing the sax than sitting at a sewing machine. He loved the idea of a formal but pliable jazz structure. Bending the basic twelve-bar outline without losing touch was the way Flower described it. Ace wanted to master the art, and he learned from Flower. After six years of practising blues-style jazz phrasing and harmony, his lithe tone on alto was getting him work, improvising in public with different musicians.

"That boy's a natural." Flower's bandleader uncle was at Meard Street, listening to the eighteen-year-old playing along to *New Orleans Blues*.

Ace had been listening to Jelly Roll Morton and his Red Hot Peppers since he was twelve, and he knew all the pianist's recorded compositions. While Ace and Pierre followed clues in London,

Flower had found treasure in America: he brought back the latest acoustical gramophone with an interior folding horn. He'd bought double-sided shellac discs of Jelly Roll's music recorded in Chicago, and one of the first jazz compositions ever published as sheet music, which happened to be *Jelly Roll Blues*. Ace played along to the 78rpm records until *King Porter Stomp* and all the other tunes were part of his repertoire.

He often thought about Zeidy while he practised. He blew hard to discharge a prickling guilt that crawled over him when he pictured the lumpy joints of his grandfather's thickening fingers. He flexed his own supple digits and ran through a cycle of fifths before coming to a decision. He'd ask his grandfather to make him a suit for his first performance at the Café de Paris; he knew Zeidy considered the Piccadilly venue respectable because the Prince of Wales was a regular visitor. With Maudie's encouragement, he'd used his charm to recover a friendship with his grandfather, though a jazz musician's life was not something Zeidy would ever take seriously.

The suit notion came back to him as he cooled down in Charing Cross Road, thinking about the debonair look of the Dixielanders in their black bow ties. He wasn't calculating; ideas occurred to him and he simply followed them through. Mostly, his cheek was endearing. At eighteen, Ace Hooker was already something of a matinee idol at the Gargoyle Club, where the bohemian regulars applauded the way he leapt on stage to give impromptu sax solos. They were persuaded by the brilliant smile, the cut of his clothes and the cast of his blueblack eyes beneath the calligraphic brushstrokes of inky brows.

He glossed and smoothed his hair with brilliantine before visiting his grandfather, and Zeidy studied him through new gold-rimmed spectacles before turning to his niece Mildred.

"See how well-groomed he is? A credit to the family."

He patted the seat beside him and Ace sat down, conscious of changes since Mildred had given up making silk undergarments at the age of twenty-six to join the tailoring business. Zeidy never allowed Bubbe to add feminine touches to his workroom, but now there were flowers on the mantelpiece and a wireless in the background playing songs from Rio Rita. Ace looked at Mildred, whose roly-poly body suggested she lived on buns.

"It keeps her happy," said Zeidy, tapping a foot. You too, thought Ace, handing him a Café de Paris handbill; the forthcoming attractions featured 'a dynamic young sax player'.

"That's you!" Zeidy took off his spectacles and polished them with a piece of chamois. "You'll be needing something smart to wear onstage if Prince Edward's there."

Mildred looked up from stitching shoulder pads into cheviot wool sleeves. "Ace would look marvellous in a white dinner jacket, don't you think?"

Zeidy grunted. "You're looking ahead to his *summer* engagements, are you?"

"Uncle, Ace would look good in one any time of the year."

Ace had vague memories of Mildred dressing him up when she looked after him as a child at Meard Street, decorating him with feathers and jewels while her big sister Annie learned to be a milliner.

Zeidy's gold-framed eyes were almost twinkling. "I'm inclined to believe a jacket in midnight blue would be appropriate."

Mildred turned and skimmed through a heap of fabric until she came to the shantung. She lifted out the bolt of heavy spun silk and held it near Ace.

"It's the colour of your eyes."

"She flatters *all* my customers." Zeidy had jumped in fast and Ace knew he was off the hook. Much better that his grandfather should be possessive about sweet-toothed Mildred than his renegade grandson. He had no interest in making suits – he simply wanted to wear them. And a jacket that matched his eyes sounded daringly debonair.

He walked along Dean Street, free from Zeidy guilt but aware of another pressure: how to earn enough money to support his club-hopping lifestyle. Zeidy was of course right – musicians were often penniless. He'd mentioned the classically trained blind violinist who played on street corners.

"Maybe he prefers performing outdoors," said Ace, and Zeidy gave him one of his shrivelling looks.

"Maybe you should open your eyes."

Flower was trying to help him join a band, but Ace wanted the freedom to link up with different musicians. He knew it was a bad time to be picky, with two million Britons unemployed, but he had to try the independent route. Pierre was going to be self-employed too. Ace stopped at the Tavern for a chat and found Pierre pacing out the empty shop next door. He was going to open it as a patisserie when he finished his pastrycook tutelage.

"The thing is," began Ace, as though they were in the middle of a conversation, "I want to be making enough money so I can always have breakfast here."

Pierre stopped pacing. "A brioche isn't going to set you back, though cocktails at the Gargoyle for all your girlfriends might empty your pockets." He started heaving furniture. "Help me move these tables. I want to see if four will fit."

They made a layout and Ace sat on one of the gilded chairs, imagining he was a customer ordering coffee and pan au chocolat. "This is going to be so mellifluous."

"So millefeuille." Pierre sat beside him. "Maybe the Café de Paris will give you a residency with your band."

"I don't have a band."

"Well, you could form one."

"No." Ace faltered. "I don't think I could manage a band. It's hard enough managing myself." He looked at Pierre with his capable pastrymaker's hands and his calm, fine-featured face – he could manage anyone.

"How about another job that fills the gaps between gigs? A friend of Papa's drives a motor cab and he earns plenty of money."

Ace grinned. He'd been having driving lessons with a friend of Annie's husband, and when he was at the steering wheel balancing pedals and gliding past horse-drawn traffic, he felt suited to it. It wasn't the rapport he experienced with his saxophone; in the driver's seat it was a connection without the rapture of music, but both activities pumped him with adrenalin.

"You're a genius, Pierre. Here you are, planning your pastry empire, and you still come up with ideas for me."

Pierre was making lists. "Shall I call it Maison Pierre?"

Ace leaned against him. "Of course. It's an impeccable name."

He left Pierre to his choux bun visions, intending to go home and learn the sax solo of a Bechet composition before anything else. He was playing *Characteristic Blues* at the Café gig in two weeks' time, accompanied by the resident pianist. When they met for rehearsals next week, Ace wanted his phrasing to be faultless.

Instead, he went to find his driving instructor Oswald ('call me Oz'), who often worked for the staff at *Vogue*, ferrying them about to fashion events in his high-topped cab. Ace's route crossed Walker's Court, and as he expected, Poppy was loitering in the street, a perky hat tipped to one side and her lipstick bold as ever. But as he came near he saw that her face was a mask of shadows.

"For the love of Harry," she croaked. "You're a sight for sore eyes."

"Who's done this to you, Poppy?" Behind the heavy makeup and the draped chiffon scarf, he could see livid bruises and throttle-marks.

"My pimp, of course. He says I'm not trying hard enough."

"That scrawny ponce?" Ace had met him once and been dismayed when Poppy introduced the pointy-faced man with dead fish eyes as her boyfriend. How could a beauty like Poppy choose a runt? She didn't explain about the boyfriend-pimp relationship until he was sixteen.

Ace looked at his hands. "I'm going to strangle *him*."

"Leave it, Ace. Nothing you can do." Her voice was hard.

"Yes, there *is* something I can do. That weasely schnorrer wastes your earnings on drink. I've often seen him at the Blue Posts, stuffing his face with Mr K's free pickles. When I tell him what's going on, Mr K will have him beaten up."

Poppy sighed. "It won't help, love. He's got friends – nasty ones – who could make trouble for your Mr K." She tried to open the clasp of her handbag to find a cigarette, but her hands were shaking.

"Mr K's son is a prize boxer, you know." Ace knew he was out of his depth, but he had to try.

Poppy gasped as she lost balance and Ace caught hold of her, feeling the chill and thinness of her body. "What can I do for you?"

"I think I need to eat something." She fumbled for her purse. "Would you buy me a sandwich?"

Ace pushed the purse away. "Come on, I'm starving too. We'll go to Abe's."

Poppy allowed herself to be led to the Wardour Street restaurant where the service was speedy and a three-course meal cost two shillings and ninepence. Ace was hungry, but Poppy's appetite was awesome. She devoured a large bowl of pea soup and a plate of roast beef while he was still eating his chopped liver starter. Spooning in the last mouthful of fruit compote, she glanced at the clock and stood up.

"Thanks Ace. Have to get back." She motioned him to stay. "Right as rain now – I won't forget this. You're a diamond."

He was paying the lunch bill when Abe the proprietor appeared from behind the waiter and muttered in his ear. "A word of advice, young Ace: that girl is trouble. Steer clear of her world."

"She's my friend," said Ace, looking up from counting out shillings, but Abe had already gone back to the kitchen.

He had to tell someone, but he didn't want to disturb Pierre in his contemplation of the perfect croissant. Would it be awkward talking to Flower about Poppy? There had been a connection between them, though it was never mentioned. Poppy had made an odd reference, but at twelve he hadn't understood the implication; he didn't know then she was a Lady of the Night, as Aaron would have put it.

She'd reckoned Ace was old enough at sixteen to know about prostitution because she'd been the same age when her 'boyfriend' put her to work on the streets of Soho. When Ace told her how his uncle would describe her, Poppy screamed with laughter.

"Me a lady? That's rich. My boyfriend has another name for me."

Thinking of her pimp, Ace pushed back the chair and bumped past startled diners bending to their soup. Outside, he breathed in traffic fumes and briefly thought about Oz the cabman before sprinting home.

Flower was there, eating a salt beef sandwich, and Maudie was at the market. Ace paced about the room.

"Something on your mind, old chap?" said Flower between mouthfuls. "Do you want a bite?"

"No, I've just had lunch with Poppy."

Flower stopped chewing and Ace waited.

"Poppy from Walker's Court?"

"Uh-huh."

"How did that come about?"

"She was fainting with hunger. Also, her despicable ponce tried to strangle her." He stared intently at Flower, who pushed his plate away and motioned Ace to sit down.

"Is she a friend of yours?" said Flower.

"Yes." Ace carried on pacing. "Is she a friend of *yours*?"

Flower raised a wiry eyebrow. "In a way, yes. Before I married your ma, Poppy was very kind to me. I didn't know how to cope as a one-legged man – as a lover, I mean. It'd been so long, and I'd lost confidence. I needed practical help, and Poppy came along at the right moment."

Ace didn't know if his stomach was twisting into a knot through envy, admiration or disgust. Flower was watching him closely, as he often did when Ace was practising the sax. But this was different – this was like an appeal for understanding.

Ace looked at his stepfather. After a long silence, he shrugged. "The thing is, how can we help Poppy?"

Chapter Fifteen

Two weeks later

It was a Wednesday when Ace hopped onto the Café's small stage in his midnight blue jacket. As he moved into the spotlight, the audience blurred before him and he expected applause, or at least silence. He heard a clatter of plates, the scrape of chairs and a buzz of conversation. He was about to be exposed as a precocious teenager and he couldn't pick out a familiar face to reassure him. He stood alone in the mauve-tinted light, listening to the wall of voices. Were they waiting for him to subdue them? He'd show them; he'd *electrify* them. Ace lifted the sax to his lips and breathed a silent incantation through the reed before launching into a Bechet classic. His fingers took on a life of their own as he blew the audience into a spellbound hush, exploring degrees of tenderness and ferocity unknown to him before. He forgot where he was and played to himself, building sounds so rich and fluid, so edgy and penetrating, that during the forty-minute set the manager made a mental note to book him for Saturday night. The audience roared for more, and after the pianist stood to applaud him and mouthed "*Potato Head Blues*?" they finished with a stirring version of the Louis Armstrong hit.

Melody Maker's jazz critic Gerry Button introduced himself. "How old are you, son?" he asked, offering his hand. "I'll be reviewing your performance in the next issue. Your sax-playing is what I'd describe as liquidly evocative."

"Thanks," said Ace. "I'm nearly nineteen."

"Shall I tell you what I'm going to say?" Mr Button didn't wait for an answer. "Ace Hooker is eighteen years old, and already he freely extends boundaries within a disciplined structure and displays an intriguing tone of compelling and unresolved tension."

The night went straight to Ace's head, and instead of going home with Flower and Maudie, he took the rickety lift to the rooftop club in Meard Street. Its mirrored walls reflected decadent glamour, and Ace wasn't surprised to be scooped up on arrival by an actress who'd watched his performance.

"Darling, you were marvellous." His face was brushed by the feathers of her headband as she stencilled his cheek with her vermilion lips.

The club owner greeted him with a champagne cocktail and offered a spin across the Channel in his Gypsy Moth. "Any talented friend of Hermione's..." he began, before being distracted by a newcomer.

An American girl in a red skirt pulled Ace onto the dance floor to jitterbug. People were flinging themselves about and Ace followed the rhythm, lulled by a cool sensation across his back until he realised a mad dancer had spilt drink over him.

In the Gents he was offered opium as he took off his jacket. "Thanks," he said "but music's my drug."

"Smart alec," said the dealer, pushing past him.

While he splashed water over the alcohol stain, Ace knew his remark would be circulating the club and they'd all know he was ignorant. But the American girl was still waiting for him. "Honey, you're dazzling!" She took him by the arm and led him towards the bar. "Do you realise everyone wants to buy you a drink for being so ironic?"

"Don't make so much noise." Ace's cracked voice came from under the blankets as Maudie came into his bedroom with a cup of tea. He heard her chuckle as she opened the shutters.

"Listen, Mr Overnight Sensation, it's midday. John has things to discuss with you and he wants you to meet him in the Tavern at one. Will you be there?"

Ace emerged from the bedclothes and cringed at the sunlight. He peered at Maudie in her shapely suit and said, "I feel wretched."

"Drink the tea. Your head may be swollen, but your body's dehydrated."

Ace levered himself up against the pillow. "Where are you going?"

"To see if my diamante order's arrived."

After she closed the door behind her, Ace tried to slip back into the golden dream he'd been having, but it was gone; all except for an image of Poppy's full red lips…Poppy! Maybe Flower had found a way of extricating her from the ponce. He crawled out of bed and swayed in circles looking for something to wear. Why was a percussion section tuning up in his head? He drank the tea and went to the bathroom.

By the time he walked into the Tavern, Ace had pulled himself together, but Pierre took one look from behind the bar and said, "You look louche, jazzman."

"A musician's prerogative," drawled Flower, clearing a space at the corner table where he'd spread himself.

Pierre looked carefully at his friend. "Go and sit down; I'll bring you a black coffee."

Ace leaned over the bar. "I did alright at the Café, didn't I?"

"Ace, you were stupendous. I told you last night, remember? Go and talk to Flower while I grind the beans."

Ace sat down beside Flower, who was making notes on a paper napkin. "Is it about Poppy?"

Flower looked surprised. "I thought we'd talk about your performance first."

"No," said Ace. "Tell me about Poppy."

"She's gone to The French Clinic for a medical, and if she's clear –"

"Clear of what?"

"VD." Flower waited a moment. "The clinic takes care of prostitutes, and if she's clear, there's a job for Poppy on a ship going to New York."

"You mean she'll leave Soho?"

"Don't sound so desolate," said Flower. "We're trying to help her."

"But I thought – I thought we could find a way of neutralising the pimp, making *him* go away so Poppy would be safe."

Flower sighed. "We don't have any influence over him, Ace, and I don't believe in strongarm tactics. "He stretched out his left leg. "Anyway, the point is, Poppy's been on the street for at least ten years. She's still in her twenties but she's already burnt out. Another job where he can't reach her is what I've been working on – am I wrong?"

Pierre was at the table with three coffees and glasses of water. "I thought I'd join you for a minute while it's quiet." He turned to Flower. "It's hard for Ace because he's been friends with Poppy since he was a little kid."

Flower watched Ace dipping sugar lumps in his coffee and eating them like sweets. "I didn't know that," he said.

"So, tell us the plan." Ace wiped his mouth with the back of his hand. "What sort of job will she have on the ship?"

"She'll work in the laundry." Flower sipped coffee. "She'll be a steam queen, travelling on one of the transatlantic liners, and if they like the way she works there'll always be a job for her."

"So Poppy will come back." Ace swung round as two men in fedoras pushed through the door; Pierre went back to the bar to serve them.

"I think there'll be a problem if she comes back to London."

"The pimp will find her," said Ace.

Flower nodded. "I think we'll have to find somewhere for her to stay in Southampton. What d'you think?"

"I think," he said slowly, "that you're trying to take control of Poppy's life."

Ace doubted himself as he saw Flower recoil. In the silence he looked across at Pierre, but he was busy chatting with the men in hats. Ace stared at Flower's bowed head of wavy hair and blinked away an image of him with Poppy. If only Flower hadn't confirmed his suspicions. Corrosion was the word, thought Ace; he was corroded by the knowledge. He'd thought he could handle it in a manly way, but he couldn't. Finding the right word only helped a bit.

"That came out wrong." He started to apologise but Flower cut him off.

"Don't say another word. Obviously you're not in a rational state to deal with practical arrangements. I've been to a lot of trouble. Bloody hell, Ace, grow up!"

Flower left the Tavern, pausing only to lean over the bar for a word with Pierre, who ducked under the counter and came to stand in front of Ace.

"Why is he so upset?" Pierre stared at his friend. "Why are *you* so upset?"

"I don't want him taking charge of Poppy's life. It makes me uneasy."

"Ace, you're jealous."

"No, I'm eaten up by knowing things about him that my ma doesn't know."

Pierre sat down beside Ace, and out of habit stacked the empty coffee cups. "Okay, so you think your innocence has been compromised, but I think there's something else."

"I just care about what happens to Poppy."

As Ace scraped back his chair in protest, a customer called for service. Pierre took the cups to the bar, and after drawing a pint of ale for the man, he called over to Ace. "Stay for lunch; Mama has Toulouse sausage."

Ace shook his head. "Tempting," he said, "but things to do." At the door he turned. "You're wrong, you know."

Ace was meeting Oz at half past two for driving practice, but the thought of Mama Pierre's meaty cassoulet nudged him into a nosh bar in Brewer Street. He sat on a high stool while the owner pushed the cigarette he was smoking to the side of his mouth and made a bulging salt beef sandwich with mustard. Ace handed over fourpence, and with an eye on the clock, wolfed down his lunch.

Oz was waiting for him outside the *Vogue* office. Walking towards him, admiring the well-fitting striped suit on the big-boned body, Ace could see Oz had picked up tips from his fashion customers.

"It's bespoke stuff, this," said Oz when Ace remarked on the cut of his clothes. "Sharp, innit?" He checked his watch. "Time to get moving."

Ace climbed into the driver's seat and squeezed the hooter. "Where to?"

"Don't go above thirty, alright? A man was killed on the road yesterday. Rozzers about; don't want to lose my licence." He settled himself into the back seat. "Regent Street first, then Selfridges. We're collecting evening frocks and bolly jackets."

"Bolero," said Ace.

"Yeah, right." Oz tapped him on the shoulder. "Concentrate on the driving and signal when you turn."

"I want to be a cab driver, Oz. What's the procedure?"

"Are you serious? I thought you were a musician."

"Can't I be both? I want to earn enough to buy a bespoke suit like yours."

"Hard graft, mate, hard graft." Oz paused while Ace changed gear. "We'll talk about it later. Let's get the job done first. Turn right and park outside the shop."

Ace swung the cab into a space and catapulted Oz from the seat as his foot slipped off the clutch.

"God's teeth," said Oz. "I'm getting out of here." He ambled off to collect samples for the *Vogue* photographer, leaving Ace to hand-wind the meter and record waiting time.

"Tell me about The Knowledge." They were drinking tea at Lyons after delivering the frocks.

"First thing to do is get yourself a bike so you can nip all over town learning routes." Oz stirred three spoons of sugar into his tea. "It's like doing a jigsaw in your brain; you build up a picture of three hundred and twenty runs, and then you fill in all the landmarks and all the attractions."

"Wherever do you start?"

"Charing Cross Station. You memorise 25,000 streets in a six-mile radius of the station – that's The Knowledge."

Ace sat back and grinned. "I can do that; I know plenty of them already."

Oz spluttered into his tea. "You're a cocky devil." He pulled out a spotted handkerchief and mopped his face. "Do you know the bridges over the Thames? Do you know all the hospitals and historic buildings? The parks? It takes two or three years to learn the lot, and by the time you take the test you'll know every club, hotel and restaurant in town, and you'll know the fastest route to each one."

"I can't wait to start." Ace pictured himself accumulating a prodigious map of his city, pedalling the streets by day on a cousin's bicycle, playing jazz into the night.

"Listen, mate," said Oz. "I know you're thinking you can bone up on all this stuff in a year – we all do – but thirty four months is the average. By the time you pass the test you'll be the right age to get a cab licence. Smart timing if you ask me."

Ace wasn't in a hurry. Lengthy apprenticeships were the fabric of his life and he could focus as long as the work charged him one way or another. He looked at Oz, with his lumpy nose and pale, protruding eyes; they hardly knew each other.

"Do you live in Soho?"

"East End's my manor. I just work here; more money in the West End, and the punters like me gabbing about the villains in Whitechapel."

Ace said, "Do you know any tough characters?"

"Like me?" Oz guffawed. "I was a bare-knuckle fighter at your age. Necessity. Had to protect myself from thugs in the neighbourhood." He held out scarred hands for inspection.

Ace stared at them. "I'm looking for someone who'll intimidate a pimp for me."

"Bloody Nora!" Oz snatched his hands out of sight and glared across the table. "What do you take me for?"

"Sorry," said Ace. "I thought..."

"You *didn't* think. You're taking liberties."

The veins in the cab driver's forehead reminded Ace of Flower's anger in the Tavern. "Listen, I don't know why I'm being so obnoxious, but I apologise. I seem to be out of kilter today."

"Is that what you call it." Oz was mollified. "Are you in trouble?"

"Not me, but..."

"Take my advice, son; don't meddle with vice. You could end up in concrete boots at the bottom of the Thames."

Ace decided Poppy was the only person who could make sense of his confusion. He couldn't reconcile his sublime jazz debut with this blundering persona. He seemed to be alienating people because of Poppy, who might have a shocking disease. He had to see her.

He turned into Walker's Court, knowing he wouldn't find her. The narrow street seemed shabbier than usual, and the fiddle music keening through the alley was unbearably apt. He looked up at Poppy's first-floor room, and her lace curtain rippled at the lopsided open window. He listened to the broken sash-cord flipping a message against the frame: I'm free, I'm free. Perhaps she was.

Ace sat on her stone step, back against the warped wood door, feet shifting over discarded cockleshells. He imagined Poppy in a starched white uniform, a Steam Queen of the open ocean, while he remained on a quayside somewhere, serenading her on the sax long after her ship had sailed. *Rhapsody in Blue*, it'd be.

He sat on the step until the blind violinist tapped along the alley and faltered at his outstretched legs. Ace got to his feet and fished in his pocket for change from his earnings the previous night. He gave the fellow musician half-a-crown. "I grew up today," he said.

Chapter Sixteen

March 1938

Ace swivelled the knob of the console to hear the news before work. He pinned the licensed driver badge to the lapel of his jacket, listening to the broadcaster's clipped voice announcing a special bulletin: volunteers were being recruited to boost the London Fire Brigade in the event of war. Ace didn't want to know about a looming war; he punched his squashed Borsalino into shape before moving to switch off the wireless. His fingers froze on the bakelite knob as the voice reported that taxis would be requisitioned to tow trailer pumps.

They're not having *my* cab, was his immediate thought.

His Austin Low Loader, parked below in the cul-de-sac curve of Meard Street, had bluegrey bodywork and a brass-mounted hooter. It represented three years of his savings topped up by a substantial gift from his Savile Row grandfather. Gramps, he knew, approved of his grandson's resourceful nature, and made it possible for Ace to move into lodgings of his own on the fourth floor. The rooms were just beneath the Gargoyle, and assuming regular's rights, Ace would climb out of his kitchen window onto the shared roof walkway and edge his way towards an emergency door into the club.

None of his fares that morning knew anything about a recruiting drive for firemen, even though one of them was an MP on his way to the Houses of Parliament. Ace stopped for elevenses at a cabbies' street canteen, and munched on a Chelsea bun while an old-timer called Sid explained what he knew.

"It's a Civil Defence precaution," he said. "If there's a war, there'll be bombs over London." He glanced at the sky for effect. "They want to create a volunteer force to fight fires because there aren't enough regular firemen."

"I heard they want to use our taxis."

"Well, if you young'uns go to war, you won't be needing your cabs for a bit, will you?"

Go to war? The man didn't know who he was talking to, thought Ace. He'd never put himself in his father's position. "Bugger that," was all he said. He crossed the road and climbed back into his cab.

He sat for some time, hands clenched on the steering wheel. He'd *never* risk exposing his weakness when other men's lives were in danger. Pierre's voice echoed in his head: 'Fear always makes you pompous, Ace'.

He turned on the engine and caused consternation as he pulled out into the path of a horsedrawn cab. Steaming off towards Victoria Station, he muttered to himself until he was flagged down outside the forecourt by a pedestrian in a bowler hat. Ace stacked the man's luggage into the space beside the driver's seat and held open the back door for him with a smile. He heard the man settle with a sigh into the cushioned leather comfort of the cab, and thought of him as sheltered from the chaos of travel, released from anxiety while this calm and capable cabbie negotiated the snarled traffic and whisked him to the Cumberland Hotel.

His next passenger was a society eccentric with a piercing voice, and unlike the previous fare, she insisted on conversation. As Ace stowed away her hat boxes, he mentioned that his mother was a milliner.

"Oh my God, Maud Lock you say? Her hats are divine!" Seeing Ace considering the construction on her head, she touched its rough texture gingerly. "This isn't one of hers, but what d'you think? Isn't it witty?"

The conical cap was made from coconut fibre and fashioned, she explained, from an African beer strainer. To wear something quite so bizarre took nerve, thought Ace. "It's inspiring," he told her. "An anomalous wonder."

He drove her to Hampstead, entertaining her with characters from the jazz world. She liked the story about the letters Louis Armstrong wrote, signing off with "Am Redbeans and Ricely Yours" or "Am Brussel Sproutsly Yours", and spent the rest of the journey composing her own. When they arrived, she tipped him generously and pecked him on the cheek.

"You're splendid company," she told him. "I'm going to invite you to my next party; Lily Shrub events are famous, y'know."

In between driving jobs he tried to think about his future. He'd established such an artful framework for himself, balancing sober days clocking up the mileage to support the wild nights jamming at clubs. A war would jeopardise everything; his structure would collapse and he'd be forced into a position where he'd disgrace himself. I'm in a funk, he told himself, watching his legs drumming against the steering wheel.

He listened like an addict to the news and only talked to Pierre once he'd made a decision. They met for a swim at Marshall Street, where they'd learned to life-save as schoolboys in the municipal pool. They dived in and raced each other for five lengths before hauling themselves out at the shallow end, wheezing.

"We're out of practice," said Pierre.

As they towelled themselves dry in the changing room, Ace

said, "I'm going to join the fire service." Beads of pool water chilled his back.

Pierre hung a towel round his neck and studied his friend. "What about your cab?"

"I'm taking it with me – they need vehicles as well."

Pierre pulled on a shirt while Ace concentrated on lacing his shoes. "It's a good move, Ace. I haven't a clue what I'll do."

"Listen, you run the best patisserie in town. Your influential customers won't let you go anywhere."

Pierre opened his mouth to speak, and closed it with a smile. The two friends exchanged looks without needing to say another word.

Three months later, on his twenty fourth birthday, Ace joined the Auxiliary Fire Service with his taxi. The undermanned London Fire Brigade gave him a rowdy welcome as one of the early volunteers, and while he learned fire fighting techniques and the dynamics of towing a 250-gallon Dennis trailer pump, his sax-playing took on a new edge. At night in the Café de Paris or the Kit-Kat, he got together with other musicians, and using only a predetermined chord sequence, they soloed against one another. Ace had the audience jumping with his blistering riffs, and the Café manager decided it was time to give Ace a lucrative residency at the club with musicians of his own choosing.

"I know it's an honour, but won't it confine me?" he asked Pierre. His friend handed him an intricate pastry from the oven.

"I offer you my fleur-de-lis speciality in recognition of your musical accolade," he said. "It's an achievement, Ace, not a sentence; celebrate!"

"Having a solid friend like you is the best achievement of my life," said Ace, and he sailed away to get himself measured for a white linen jacket.

The AFS uniforms, when they were issued a year later, were sturdy and workmanlike, but with the ranks swelled to fourteen thousand, there weren't enough to go round. Ace volunteered to wear a surplus postman's outfit to go with his steel helmet and respirator; the important element of the uniform for him was the star-shaped badge he pinned to the tunic. He was part of a service that was independent of all the British armed forces, and if 'army dodger' snipes came his way he planned to say, "I'm a neutral fireman – I'll save anyone in trouble."

August 1939

Two thousand requisitioned taxis were being painted battleship grey. Ace watched his cab becoming an anonymous part of the fleet until voices made him turn. He looked round at a girl with large brown eyes.

She was with a group of women recruits, sent to find patrol officer Ace who was in charge of training new staff and teaching driving skills.

"Did you say something?"

"I was asking if I'd be allowed to drive one of them," said the brown-eyed girl. She pointed to the grey fleet.

Ace looked at her; extremely pretty, he gauged, even in a lumpy boiler suit with a scarf knotted round her head.

"I've come straight from the factory," she said. "I can't go through the war being a riveter." Her voice had a lilt.

"What do you rivet?"

"Wing-flaps for Beaufort fighters. It was a kettle factory before." She pulled off the scarf and shook out soft curly hair. "My name's Kitty."

"Come with me Kitty," he said. "There's a job for you driving a canteen van – two pounds a week till the war's over."

Kitty frowned. "I thought the Home Office said they were paying three pounds."

"That's what the men are getting. Sorry."

Kitty shrugged. "Business as usual then."

She fell into step with him as they crossed the yard to a makeshift office. "You are over seventeen, aren't you?" he asked, looking for the forms.

"I'm twenty-one and fit for anything," said Kitty. "Will I be working in the canteen as well?"

"Do you want to?"

"Of course! I'm a dab hand at pies and puddings. I love cooking, and I want to drive so I can be near the action. I want to be useful."

Ace looked into Kitty's burnt sienna eyes. You can have anything you want, he thought. "Let's show you how to drive then," he said.

The canteen vans were heavy and erratic to handle, but Kitty had strong arms and quick reactions. She also had a knack for listening to Ace as though he was imparting words of incalculable value. He sat in the passenger seat absorbing her factory-scarred hands at the wheel, her diligent profile, the slight jut of a front tooth, the raised mole behind a perfect ear. He wanted to kiss that earlobe.

She braked suddenly to avoid a child running over the road, and Ace lurched towards the windscreen, relieved he hadn't had time to make a fool of himself.

"That's the emergency stop I was going to teach you!" He rubbed his head and turned to her. "Are you alright?

"Bit shaken up," she whispered.

He looked at his watch. "We'll stop now. Come back tomorrow and I'll show you how to manoeuvre out of a tight spot."

Kitty made no comment, though she leaned on his arm when he helped her out of the van. Ace watched her leave the fire station, walking with a slight pigeon-toed turn of the feet.

There was a message from her next morning that she was obliged to do two more days at the factory, and when she reappeared at the end of the week, Ace hovered in the office doorway, absorbing the way she moved across the yard towards him with that hobbled walk of hers. He took her over to the canteen van, and as she was about to start the engine he noticed a ring on her left hand.

"Why were you hiding it?" He stared at the tiny winking diamond.

"Oh, I forgot to take it off. I don't wear it when I'm working." Kitty folded the ring into a handkerchief and put it in her pocket. "What's it to you, anyway?"

"I'm surprised, that's all. Flabbergasted!" He clowned astonishment to mask his dismay, and when she smiled he fixed her with his dark seductive eyes.

"Of course you've been snapped up, Kitty. Who's my rival?"

"Your what?" Kitty giggled. "Shall I start the engine now?"

"No, wait," said Ace. "This is serious, Kitty. I want to know who bought you that fancy ring."

"His name's Edgar," said Kitty. "Now please will you show me how to reverse this van."

She wouldn't answer anymore questions until she'd practised three-point turns, hill starts and reversing into a tight space. Ace looked at her triumphant face and said, "Does Eddie know how lucky he is?"

"Eddie?" Kitty smirked. "He doesn't like nicknames."

"Takes himself seriously, does he, your paramour?"

Kitty's laughter brought to mind a pebbled brook of spring water.

"My fiancé's a serious bank clerk if you must know. A man with prospects, he says."

"Is that why you're marrying him?"

"My father tells me not to be pert when I ask rude questions like that."

Ace couldn't be sure if he'd detected a gleam in her eye. "I'm intrigued," he said. "Won over by your prevaricating tactic." He opened the window beside him to let in air. "Does your father approve of Eddie?"

"When you meet him, you mustn't call him that," she said. "He'll have enough trouble accepting *your* funny name."

"Fair enough," said Ace. "I'll address him as Mr – ?"

"Spigot."

"SPIGOT?" Ace thumped the dashboard and roared with laughter. "I can't let you marry him; Kitty Spigot sounds like a plumber's tool."

"Funnily enough, my dad's a plumber's merchant. He's got a shop in Holborn." Kitty gave him a cool look. "You wouldn't be suggesting I'd be better off with a name like yours, would you?"

Mischievous wench, thought Ace. I've met my match here. He hadn't been bothered by American jazzmen using his surname to refer to prostitutes, but of course his future wife might be sensitive.

"Whatever gave you that idea?" he said, and couldn't resist kissing her hot cheek before she forced open the van door and stormed away.

September 1939

He wasn't getting anywhere with Kitty. She was a dutiful daughter of conventional parents, and they forcefully approved of Edgar and his prospects. Decent and dogged, Ace imagined him, and it was up to him to show Kitty that life with Ace would be a far richer experience, even with a war on. He was telling her as much as they stood in Broadwick Street, checking the water level of a 5,000 gallon tank stationed there for firebomb raids.

"You'll be exhilarated!" he said, when simultaneously the first air-raid siren of the war went off. Kitty looked at him as though he was some sort of deity and Ace made a note of the time – 11.27am – as they sped towards their posts. In broad daylight, he stumbled into a street lamp painted with white stripes for the blackout.

The siren was a false alarm and the pumped up fire crews eventually drifted off to play snooker and darts. While Ace potted balls, he decided on his first date with Kitty: he'd take her to watch the best swing band in the country.

"How do you know that?" challenged Kitty when he shared his plan with her.

"Wait and see," said Ace. "Snakehips is unforgettable."

"Snakehips! What sort of a name is *that*?"

"When you see him dance you'll understand."

"But we'll be on call tonight," said Kitty.

"We'll tell a bike messenger how to find us if there's an emergency." His voice was soothing. "We will be safe," he said, "because the club's in a basement; four storeys of masonry above as protection."

Kitty still hesitated and Ace was scrabbling. "What will Eddie do if there's a raid tonight?"

"He'll go to Holborn underground, I suppose."

"And we'll be at the fire station getting our orders."

He'd clinched it, and that night they slipped through the unlit streets like curfew-busters. Taxis with masked headlamps flickered by and a prostitute in Piccadilly illuminated her presence with a candle held between cupped palms. Kitty drew close to link arms with Ace, and he realised he was holding his breath as her broad warm hip nudged his leg.

"Ken Johnson and his Rhythm Swingers," Kitty read out as they approached the Café de Paris entrance. "Nothing about Snakehips."

"That's the bandleader's nickname," said Ace. "Come on, they've started."

They pushed through the door to see a flexible young man with cinnamon skin swing his band into *Sunny Side of the Street*.

Saturday 7th September 1940

Ace was on the early shift. The first thing he heard as he changed was *Snakehips Swing*; Kitty was singing in the mobile canteen where she brewed tea for the crew. He'd bought the record for her to play on the portable gramophone she kept in a leatherette case. He listened to her voice; so pure he was lured over to the van.

"Please let me hear you say you love me." He heard himself babbling like a B-movie actor.

Kitty was standing at the serving hatch, lining up china cups on the counter with methodical fingers. She stopped what she was doing, and Ace had the impression that her body was filling with a glorious stillness. Her eyes glistened, but she said nothing. He leaned on the counter and watched her measure out tea for the pot.

"You're making me nervous," she said. "Haven't you got a fire to put out?"

Ace bent to kiss her arm, bare below rolled-up overalls, and Kitty jerked a spoonful to the floor. "Now look," she wailed. "I'm spilling precious rations, and there goes your cup of tea."

He stepped away from the van, hands up in mute surrender. "Come to the park with me after work," he said.

"Only if you stop badgering me."

Ace couldn't remember when he felt like this. Yes he could: with Poppy. His first love, though he'd never told her. And then she sailed away and never came back.

They walked to Green Park in sunshine that afternoon, and lay on the grass close together looking up at barrage balloons in a summer sky.

"You are my darling dirigible," said Ace, "but I'm damned if I know how to dislodge that wretched ring from your finger."

He sat up, ears straining. "Your Mr Spigot..." he was saying, before sirens obliterated the rest of his words.

"On with yer battle bowlers," yelled the senior officer. Ace ran to his locker, and drilled into expectations of falling shrapnel and drops of blister gas, he pulled on a tin helmet. He dragged oilskins over his trousers and looped a gas mask round his neck.

Every fire appliance in London was heading for the docks, Ace and his team in his camouflaged taxi, with a ladder on the roof and a trailer pump behind. It seemed obscene to be thrilled by an air-raid; did soldiers feel like this going into battle? He glanced round at the other three and saw their eyes were fever-bright too.

Strange odours reached his nostrils before he saw the devastation. A spice warehouse was exploding as they arrived, and plumes of pepper dust stung his eyes while they uncoiled the hoses. Ace concentrated on containing the blaze before daring to take in the scale of the job ahead: fires were raging in oil depots and chemical works, and the dock basin itself was a sea of liquid fire, fuelled by rum and sugar spewing from bombed warehouses. The unseemly thrill evaporated.

When the all-clear sounded sixty minutes later, it dawned on Ace that German bombers had been flying overhead while he was crouched below. Why hadn't he been aware of them? His hose was trained on a paint factory, he knew the mains had been ruptured and that river water was being relayed from barges on the Thames, four tonnes a minute; that was his focus. But it was odd not to have seen one.

Two hours later the bombers were back, flying in formation with a fighter escort, moving upriver, circling the docks and dropping bombs across the whole of East London. Ace saw them this time. He roared himself hoarse, coughing up black gobs of hot dust; he was still searching for survivors from the first raid.

Chapter Seventeen

The Blitz 1940

Ace had never seen a dead body. He hoped the training would back him up when the time came; he sensed the time *had* come when the Royal Arsenal blew up. Teams of firemen were positioning themselves to swamp the flames before they engulfed the ammunition stores, while Ace was among the crew directed to the dockland street where a row of terraced houses had been flattened. He was to find survivors and lead them to the evacuation boats.

Standing on the rubble of one home, he saw that his rubber boot was brushing against the fingers of a hand; an open hand, palm up. He bent and lifted away bricks, one by one, until he could see the hand was detached. He noted the plain wedding band on a knobbly finger, and slipped the hand into his pocket. He couldn't just leave it there.

His mind was on the evacuees, bereaved and homeless, and later, the fire he was called to at a dockside rubber factory belching flames and toxic black smoke. And then a food warehouse, where sacks of grain burst open in the deluge and the drains blocked up with swollen rice.

"Am I hallucinating?" he asked a colleague many hours later when the waterlogged road under his feet started heaving. And when the all-clear sounded at five in the morning, a telegraph pole burst into flames. Ace slid to the ground and sagged against the wheel of a trailer pump, wild laughter exploding from his spent body. His nose was so bunged up he couldn't breathe properly, and he reached in his pocket for a rag to wipe away the muck.

Kitty found him holding the severed hand when she drove to the docks at dawn.

"Someone may be missing this," said Ace.

Kitty gagged at the sight of the blackened hand. "Missing it?"

"The ring, I mean. If she's still alive."

"Yes, of course." Kitty became brisk. "I'm sure there are wardens for this area; I expect they'll be able to help."

Ace was staggering to his feet. "You're exhausted," she said. "Why don't you rest for a bit? I'll find a warden when the tea's made. We've got extra rations of sugar lumps."

"Must tell the boss or someone will think I'm pilfering valuables." He veered away, calling out, "Tea with lots of sugar, please."

Kitty and the canteen crew were parked in a clearing beside a bombed bakery. The baker had been pulled alive from the wreckage, and firemen were still salvaging trays of loaves from the solid brick oven.

"Want to buy some Conflagration Bread for the bacon butties?" a fireman asked the women.

"It's perfect!" Kitty was examining a loaf. "Yes, if it helps the poor baker, we'll have a trayful. You must all be famished."

For the next three hours, Kitty served tea, made thick sandwiches and prepared a meal of corned beef hash with carrots. She noticed her engagement ring was spattered with gravy, and dabbed it with a teacloth before slipping the ring into her purse. A vision of that married hand came to mind, and it occurred to Kitty that if she were to die in this war, she'd rather not be found wearing Edgar's ring; it would give the wrong impression.

She had loved Edgar for his unshakeable clarity of purpose, and also for the symmetry of his film star face, but since his rejection by the army for the second time, she'd been delaying their wedding plans.

"I've got a heart murmur," he told Kitty.

"Is that bad?"

"Bad enough for the orderly to say the training would probably kill me before I got to the battlefield. He called me mate!"

"I expect he was trying to be friendly," said Kitty. "Will you have to have an operation?"

"I was born with it, they think. I have to avoid strenuous exercise, that's all."

Kitty was supportive, but Edgar's anxiety about his heart condition exaggerated his alarm for her safety.

"I want you to give up this fire service work," he said. "It's time for us to be married and move to the country. You'll be able to keep chickens and grow vegetables, and I'll work my way up to be bank manager of the local branch."

Kitty could see the sense in this even as her own heart murmured 'no'. She'd been non-committal, but now she was clear: she'd hand back the diamond solitaire and tell him. She'd say, "I can't marry you Edgar, you know that. I'd suffocate in the country. I want to be in the middle of it all – whatever the risk. I don't want to be mollycoddled."

What she wouldn't say was that she'd fallen in love with Ace.

Kitty thought about this while she dissolved milk powder into a jug of water for bread pudding. After her first week at the fire station, she'd told her sister about the man who was teaching her to drive.

"He's a saucy fellow," she said. "Full of cheek, but he does make me laugh."

"What does he look like?" her sister wanted to know.

"Virile," said Kitty, and her sister was thrilled. "Gordon Bennett! Better not mention him to Edgar, then." And Kitty hadn't.

She'd had her doubts about Ace anyway; she thought he was flighty. All the night-clubbing was frivolous, and the gigs where he wore that fancy white jacket and blew his sax in such a way that she wanted to behave like a slut and be ravaged by him…Kitty the virgin was scandalised by her response to his music. Once, after playing *Body and Soul*, Ace had come off stage slick with sweat and gathered her into a steamy embrace, and Kitty had leaned into his fruity armpit and breathed the smell of heaven. It was all magical, but where was the substance?

Only now, in the blitz, did she detect a scrupulous side to Ace, and his respect for human remains convinced her: Ace was the man for Kitty.

She scattered sultanas between layers of buttered bread and poured over the milk mixed with sugar and egg powder. She set the pie tins aside to let the bread soak, and stepped out of the van to find her man.

An air-raid warden had identified the hand as belonging to his neighbour's dead wife.

"I'll tell the fireman who found it," said Kitty, handing him a cup of tea.

"Parched, I am," he said, and Kitty noticed his frizzled eyebrows and blistering cheeks. He blew on the cup. "George is going to take this badly."

"George?"

"Lilian's husband. George called her a skinny bitch but he thought the world of her." The warden gulped tea. "She managed their five kids *and* brought in ninepence a week as a knocker-up."

"What's that?" said Kitty.

"Bit of a speciality round here," he said. "She'd shoot dried peas at bedroom windows to wake dockers for the dawn shift. Worked a treat; she aimed sharp with that peashooter."

"You'll give her husband the ring, won't you?"

"Aye. Lil thought it was real gold, bless her, but George won it at a fair."

Kitty took his empty cup and the warden adjusted his tin helmet. She willed him to be gone. Where was her man? She wanted to clear the delusions from her life.

He'd been sent home to sleep after a twelve-hour shift, and now he was in Maison Pierre's eating an off-ration meal of scrambled eggs. He kept glancing at his friend, clearing crockery from tables in a preoccupied state. Ace waited till he was the only customer in the patisserie.

"Talk to me," he said.

"I can't say much," said Pierre, "but if I suddenly disappear, don't be alarmed."

Ace locked eyes with his friend. "I'm alarmed just hearing you say that."

Pierre went to the street door and locked it, hanging the closed sign in the window. He sat down opposite Ace. "Enough butter in the eggs?"

"Delicious, and I don't take it for granted, but this is a diversionary tactic."

"Well," said Pierre, "if I'm not here one of these days, I'll be in France. I've joined the resistance."

"Of course! I knew you'd get involved in something clandestine."

Pierre pressed a finger to his lips. "You mustn't mention this to *any*one Ace, but it is a relief to tell you."

"Can you say more? I want to know how you got involved."

"Through Papa, really. Remember I told you about his political friend doing a BBC broadcast?"

"I listened to it," said Ace. " It confused me."

"France has surrendered and his government's collapsed," said Pierre. "De Gaulle's been tried in his absence and found guilty of treason."

"What's the sentence?"

"Death."

"Where is he now?"

Pierre gestured with his eyes.

"In the *Tavern*. My god, Pierre, the resistance movement's next door?"

"Keep your voice down Ace. We're the Free French group, and I'll prob'ly be a courier."

Ace stared at his friend. "No wonder you've been making fleur-de-lis pastries, you patriot."

Pierre shook his head. "I only made them to welcome Papa's friend to London."

"Patriotism is overrated if you ask me," said Ace.

"If you ask me," said Pierre, "I'd say you were becoming political."

Ace grinned. "Steady on, I'm a neutral fireman." After a moment he said, "Did you hear that Gramps' neighbour Giovanni's been interned?"

"An enemy alien, is he?"

"He's a tailor!"

"Then they prob'ly think he's been stitching secret documents into coat linings." Pierre's laugh was strained.

Ace looked at his watch and stood up. "I've got to go and teach street fire parties how to use stirrup pumps."

Pierre went to the door and unlocked it. "The Tavern used to be in German hands before the last war, you know. Herr Schmidt was the publican until he was sent to an internment camp; that's when Papa took over."

They lingered in the doorway. "Am I supposed to make sense out of what you just said?"

"No," said Pierre. " I was thinking aloud. We're all individuals and we do what we can. But the borders keep shifting so we can't take anything for granted."

Ace shut his eyes. "In a world of shifting borders / Where deranged men give the orders..." His eyes snapped open.

"The lyrics for your next song?"

"Maybe," said Ace. "Can you hear the plangent sax?"

Pierre nodded. "I'll come to the premiere."

"That word 'deranged' – does it give you the creeps?"

Pierre shrugged. "It's a powerful word – well-chosen, I'd say."

They clasped hands and turned from each other. Ace walked away fast, though he wasn't late.

Kitty sped along High Holborn towards her father's shop. Her laboured breathing was more to do with Edgar than exertion. She'd gone to the bank where he worked to hand back the ring, and his response had left her winded.

"Like vermin leaving a sinking ship," he'd said, crushing the diamond into his fist. "I confide in you about my weak heart and you give up on me, is that it? I could die anytime, but you're indifferent."

"Edgar, that's unfair. Any one of us could die in an instant; that's not the point."

"The point is, Kitty, you see me as a cripple, don't you?"

In a way he was right, she thought miserably, gazing at a handsome face pinched by events.

"I don't want a compromised life," said Kitty, "and if that sounds harsh, then you know I'm not the wife for you."

Edgar stood up, slowly opened his fist and watched the ring drop to his desk. "Leave," he said, without raising his eyes. "I can't bear to look at you for another minute."

So Kitty left, deciding to tell her parents before doubt skewed her judgement. "I feel despicable," she told them, "but I wouldn't make Edgar happy."

Her father put down the copper joints he was sorting and patted her shoulder. "Don't be hard on yourself, lovey. Edgar was never going to amount to much with a dicky heart like that. I said as much to your mother, didn't I, Ethel?"

Ethel nodded, and gave her daughter a peck on the cheek before going back to the accounts. "Sorry love," she said, "but I've got to finish them before we go to the shelter. Dot's already there if you want to see her."

Kitty's sister was guarding a place for the family at Holborn Station. It was four o'clock, and already most of the platforms and passage space had been reserved with bedrolls. Kitty walked along the white line three feet from the edge of the rails, where passengers were lining up for the next train.

"It's stuffy down here." Kitty sat beside her sister on a blanket folded against the wall.

"Safe as houses though," said Dot, and sniggered. "I mean, safe as a bunker." She laid aside the magazine she was reading and passed Kitty a flask. "Have a nip – you look peaky."

Kitty took a swig and sighed. "Brandy! You know how to live underground."

"It makes a change from working in the shop all day," said Dot. "There's talk of a concert down here next week if the bombing goes on."

Kitty looked at her placid sister. "I told Mum and Dad I'm not going to marry Edgar and they weren't at all bothered. I thought they'd be livid."

"They'll be relieved," said Dot. "They were frantic about the expense of a wedding; they thought Edgar would expect a good show." She tucked *Picturegoer Weekly* under her pillow as a train blew into the station. "How did poor Edgar take it?" she shouted.

"Badly," mouthed Kitty.

After the train had gone, she stood up. "Have to check the canteen's stocked for tomorrow."

"What about the Virile Fireman? Have you checked up on him?"

"Mind your own business, Nosy Sis." Kitty retraced her steps to the exit, telling herself the next siren would bring them together if her feet didn't stray off the white line.

A black taxi drew level with Ace as he made his way to the fire station in Shaftesbury Avenue. Glimpsing a familiar tuberous nose, he leaned into the cab and shook the driver's thick hand.

"Oz, my old pal, where have you been?"

"Ducking and diving, mate. Sculling about."

"Any bomb damage to your place? I was thinking about you the other night."

"All hunky-dory," said Oz. "Jump in; where are you going?"

"There." Ace pointed to the fire station ahead.

"Expecting a raid tonight?"

"We're on full alert," said Ace, "but I'm not on duty till six."

"Time for a bevy then. My shout."

Oz parked opposite the station by a bar that operated from its cellar at night and specialised in brown ale and extra-strong porter. He brought two tankards of stout to a beer barrel table and offered a toast.

"To the Windmill Girls – may they never be stopped!"

"I'll drink to that," said Ace, "but you're being obscure."

Oz raised an eyebrow. "You don't know about them? My niece is one of the chorus girls. The idea is they do non-stop revues all through the war. They won't stop for anything; not unless they're bombed to buggery."

"Is that where you've been today, with your niece?"

Oz nodded. "Don't get to see her otherwise. She more or less lives at the theatre; they sleep in the dressing rooms, down in the basement."

"To the dancing girls," said Ace, tipping malty liquor down his throat. He wiped foam from his mouth. "Is there any other reason you go there?"

"Squire! What do you take me for?"

"A vigorous widower who'd like romance."

"You're a canny bugger," said Oz. "Well, there *is* this gorgeous girl I've got friendly with. She's a fan dancer. I thought one of the men in the troupe was her boyfriend, but it turns out he's a ginger beer, so I'm in with a chance."

Ace picked up his tankard. "I wish you luck, pal. I'm still trying to persuade Kitty I'm the love of her life."

"Don't know why any doll would hesitate with a geezer like you," said Oz. "Me, I'm an ugly brute, though I know how to make a girl laugh."

The sirens wailed as they made their way up to the street.

"Where are you off to now?" said Ace.

"Westminster." Oz opened his cab door. "Plenty of work at Parliament, and if I keep the politicians sweet they're more likely to raise the petrol ration for taxis."

"You're the canny one," said Ace.

"Come and see the show; come to the late matinee tomorrow."

"I will." Ace waved and sprinted across the road to assemble his kit.

He attached a waterproof neck protector to his helmet, thinking about the Windmill. He didn't know why he'd agreed to go; the song and dance numbers weren't stimulating, and the motionless poses of the glamorous nudes were strangely deflating. More than anything, after a night of firefighting, he wanted to be with Kitty. He wanted her steady brown eyes on him as he peeled off her clothes. He wanted to see *her* naked body; he wanted to feel her yielding voluptuously while he kissed every particle of her. He…

"Come on dozy, there's a war on." His team were jostling round him.

"Chop-chop, Hooker." They hustled him out to his taxi.

They reached the docks to be confronted by flames rising a hundred feet from the wharf, where a consignment of pine and fir timber had caught fire. Ace parked by a railway arch sheltering Silvertown residents, and their cheering gave the firemen a boost as they drenched all the wooden structures nearby before turning to the inferno. Ace wrapped his arms round a hose, bracing it against his thigh, while Mac directed the nozzle. Incendiaries spun round them and splinters of burning wood floated their way while they tried to contain the blaze and save the wharf. Ace blinked hard to clear his eyes; through columns of smoke he detected smouldering sugar barges drifting past, trailing burnt mooring ropes and a stench of caramel.

"Hey!" A jet of water hit him in the face as the nozzle escaped from Mac's hands; a bomb had dropped directly into the fire they were putting out.

Mac was on his back. Ace hung onto the rearing hose yelling "Knock off! Knock off the water!" to the man at the pump. When the hose went limp, he ran to his colleague and pulled him clear, understanding the meaning of a dead-weight.

"Where's your helmet gone?" he said to no-one, noticing Mac's ginger head had changed shape. A man ducked out from the arch and dropped to his knees beside Ace.

"I'm a doctor," he said, checking for a pulse. He shook his head and put a thin blanket in Ace's hands before doubling back to the shelter.

Ace straightened the splayed limbs and wiped blood from the AFS badge on Mac's tunic, remembering their conversation from the night before.

"It's my wee shield," Mac had said, and Ace went still, recognising the sentiment.

"Protecting you from what?"

Mac studied the ground. "From shaming myself on the battlefield."

"Exactly what I fear," said Ace.

Mac looked at him. "I'm afeared I wouldn't be brave."

"Me too," said Ace.

He pulled the blanket over the man who'd died with their secret. "No reason to be afeared now," he whispered.

Over fifty-seven consecutive nights of bombing, Ace came to the conclusion that at least he was up to this job. He volunteered to enter burning buildings, and led trapped occupants to safety. He scaled fire ladders to rescue people, and he didn't disgrace himself when he helped rescue workers fill rubble baskets with charred body parts.

"What happens to them?" he asked the driver as he stacked baskets into an ambulance.

"We take them to the municipal swimming baths. The pool's been drained, and people from the mortuary lay all the parts on the floor and try, like, to piece them together."

Ace came off duty wanting the wholeness of Kitty, but his shifts ended as hers began, and their days off hadn't coincided. He checked the station rota and found one daytime slot when they'd both be free: he'd take her to a concert, and if she wasn't wearing creepy Ed's ring, he'd propose they got married immediately.

The Windmill Theatre event had stirred him more than he expected. The show hadn't moved him, but afterwards Oz had taken him to the fan dancer's dressing room where he'd met her friend Elsie. She had long honey-toned legs and a playful smile.

"You fancied young Elsie, didn't you?" said Oz when they left.

"Those legs!" said Ace.

Chapter Eighteen

1940-41

Kitty stopped on a temporary bridge spanning Charing Cross Road and stared into the bomb crater below. It occurred to her that it was an odd time to be shopping for clothes, but she'd heard there were bargains to be had in Oxford Street. Ace had left her a note in the canteen van, and she wanted something new to wear when she met him.

"You're not avoiding me are you, Kitty?" he'd written in his invitation to an open-air concert in Trafalgar Square.

She stuck a reply on his locker: "Far from it!! Meet me at Nelson's Column if it's still standing." She hoped the perky style masked a sudden shyness at being single again.

She stepped over shattered plate glass in search of a pretty blouse. Whole shop fronts in the West End had been blown out, but business was brisk at a wrecked department store where salesgirls had set up a makeshift counter on the pavement. Kitty climbed over fallen masonry and eased her way through a scrum of customers to a table of salvaged lingerie. She picked out a lilac chemise and examined it for damage.

"There's just a speck of soot on the hem." A salesgirl pointed out a smudge on the lace. "It'll wash out and be good as new."

"Your sweetheart won't notice it anyway," said a voice behind Kitty, and she whirled round to face her gleeful sister.

"Are you snooping on me, Dot?"

"Don't need to, Kitty. I come here, all innocent, looking for a stocking kit, and I find my big sister buying herself risky clothing!"

"I haven't bought anything yet," said Kitty.

"Well, get a move on and buy that satin slip before someone else snaps it up; the Virile Fireman's going to love it."

Kitty opened her purse. "Why am I cursed with such a vulgar sister?"

"Because," said Dot, "without me you'd have no-one to egg you on when you want to be a devil. Now help me find a kit for my legs."

Kitty looked at her sister's perfectly arched eyebrows. "Why don't you use your face makeup? Put foundation on your legs first and then draw seams down the back with an eyebrow pencil."

"Is that a utility fashion tip?" said Dot.

"It is," said Kitty. "And in exchange, I want you to lend me your best suit."

From the base of Nelson's Column, Ace watched Kitty make her way towards him across the square, noticing how that bird-toed walk made her rounded hips sway with every step.

"You are mesmerising, my darling Kittywake," he said, when she stood before him. She was skewering a loose pin back into the little hat perched on the side of her piled up curls. He reached for her hands, and without taking his eyes off her bright face, established she was ring-free and available.

"Marry me, Kitty." The words popped out and took them both by surprise.

"Damn," he said. "I meant to ask you after the concert. I was going to introduce you to my parents first; give you a clue about my intentions."

He squeezed Kitty's hands. Her lips were parted, but she hadn't uttered a word, and her brown eyes were distant. He kissed the tips of her fingers, and when her eyes focused he sat her on the wall of the square's empty fountain.

"I've shocked you with my blundering proposal," he said. "Forgive me for being a silly bugger; I'm going to do it properly now."

Kitty tugged on his arm to stop him kneeling. "Ace, my own sweet bugger, I *will* marry you."

"You will?" He searched her face for delayed shock symptoms and saw that her eyes were about to flood.

"Of *course* I'll marry you. These are tears of joy."

Ace lifted her into his arms, experiencing a timid sense of gratitude to Kitty before the flash of victory – he'd saved her from Edgar!

"Darling girl," said Maudie, when Ace introduced his bride-to-be. His mother had slipped away from making parachutes to be at the lunchtime concert, intrigued by her son's insistence. She sat Kitty beside her in the semi-circle of seats set up for the open-air event while Ace went to find Flower. He'd joined the big band to play *Smoke Gets In Your Eyes* to blitzed Londoners. A spontaneous carnival atmosphere was attracting jugglers and food vendors to the square, and once the concertgoers discovered the groom-to-be was related to the sax player, Ace and Kitty were swept to the front seats with Maudie, and the band played *Happy as the Day is Long*.

"Come home with me," Ace whispered in Kitty's ear, and while the audience applauded the show, they slipped away to Meard Street.

"Could you live here, Kitty?"

"I could," said Kitty, "as long as it's with you."

Ace mixed them pink gins and played *Snakehips Swing* on the gramophone. Kitty jiggled to the music, and when she slipped off her shoes he pulled her to the couch. Holding her feet, he drew her toes into his mouth, one at a time, until she was slithering in his arms. Ace was sliding his hands over the salvaged chemise when Kitty pushed away.

"We mustn't, Ace. I'd feel so guilty. Please let's get married as soon as possible." She reached for her jacket. "Am I being silly?"

"You're being excruciatingly rational," said Ace, crushing her to his heart. "Feel it? It's beating arhythmically for you."

"Mine too," said Kitty, "but please let's wait."

"You've bewitched me with your wholesomeness." He released her and bent double, groaning. "We'll wait because my love for you is not a shallow thing; it's an immense shaggy bear of devotion."

Two days before the wedding, Ace was called to a fire in Coventry Street. High-explosive bombs were dropping over Piccadilly Circus and Leicester Square, and one of them had crashed through the roof of the Rialto Cinema into the basement club below.

"The Café de Paris?"

"Yup," said the senior officer, and Ace yelled for his crew to get cracking. It was 9.30pm and the resident band would have started their set, led by Ken Snakehips Johnson. Why had Snakehips changed the name of his group to The West Indian Dance Band? It nagged at Ace that he didn't know.

"Come on, lads," he snapped, as they uncoupled the pump and backed it into the kerb outside the cinema.

"Steady on, Hooker," said Starky. "Lead the way. We're right behind you."

They pulled out rolls of hose, and the pumpman attached a length to a hydrant and tightened the suction lugs while the others hauled their equipment into the building. They manhandled the hose through the stairwell, coupling lengths together as they went.

The bomb had travelled four storeys down an airshaft and smashed through a glass ceiling into the club. Before they reached the bottom of a narrow stone stairway, Ace knew it would have exploded on the dance floor. The club was small, but Snakehips was a magnet for the swing set and he reckoned at least a hundred people would be trapped down there. They shouldered their way through jammed doors and stood on the threshold, choking. The ambulance crew were waiting above until the fire was out, and in the confined space, Ace and Starky manoeuvred the hose over a turmoil of dead and injured patrons. All around them on the dance floor, voices begged for help.

"Jesus!" Starky staggered as a hand from the mass grabbed his ankle. Behind him Ace could see his heavy colleague was losing his balance. He dived forward and unlocked the fingers, looking into the terrified eyes of a woman covered in blood.

"Lady, we'll help you in a minute," said Starky. "We're putting out the fire first."

"Am I hurt? Is it my blood?" she was saying, over and over again.

"Water!" yelled Ace, and listened to the call being relayed up to the pumpman in the street. The crew braced themselves as the limp hose began to writhe. Ace could hear the nozzle in Starky's hands singing like a kettle and he stiffened as the water came roaring through. He heaved against it to control the back thrust of pressure. Water squirted in his face and up his sleeves – always up his sleeves – and he reached for the spanner in his belt to tighten a leaking joint.

When the fire was under control and the first stretchers arrived, Ace knelt beside a sobbing girl whose legs were pinned by a girder.

"Have you free in a jiffy," he told her.

"I can't feel them," she whimpered. "I won't be able to dance again!"

"I'm sure you will," said Ace, thinking of Flower. He levered the beam off her crushed knees and she started to scream. He stayed with her until a doctor gave her morphine, and she went limp sighing, "*Oh Johnny.*"

Ace leapt to his feet and made for the stage. He knew some members of the band had been taken to Charing Cross Hospital, but what had happened to their swivel-hipped young leader?

Among the debris of crushed instruments he found Snakehips, so composed in death he looked asleep. Ace could find no visible damage. The smooth-skinned face was serene; even the flower in his lapel was fresh. He leaned in close, but there was no breath to warm his cheek.

He rocked on his heels, considering; unstable walls might collapse anytime. He looked around for a spare stretcher, but a man with a head wound was being carried away on the last one, and the firemen were calling him as they hauled out their equipment to make way for the Suicide Squad on unexploded bomb duty.

"One more to bring out," shouted Ace, lifting Snakehips over his shoulder; he couldn't leave him there.

When he reached the street and laid the musician on the pavement, an ambulanceman came over to examine the patient. "Sorry mate, he's gone."

Ace nodded. He crouched beside the body and saw he'd crushed the button-hole on the way up; he lifted the flower from Snakehips' lapel and pocketed the petals.

The night watch arrived to take over and the crew drove back to the station, leaving Ace to walk home.

"I need to clear my head," he told them. "That was a weird thing I did."

"No mate," said Starky. "You knew him."

"But he was already dead!"

Starky shrugged. "No harm done. Get some sleep – you're knackered."

Ace trudged along Great Windmill Street and was suddenly engulfed by jolly theatregoers emerging from a show. They made way for him, the stark-eyed fireman with ash in his hair, as he strode towards the stage door. The doorman could see Ace wasn't one of the Stagedoor Johnnies trying to get the knickers off a dancer with a box of chocolates, and he went to fetch Elsie.

"Someone to see you, urgentlike," he told her, and still in her Polynesian outfit, Elsie ran up the stairs in a panic.

"What is it?" Her voice shot up a register seeing chaos in a fireman's eyes.

"All well," said Ace. "Everything alright. Bombs down the road. Came to see you were okay."

Elsie's eyes shone. "Oh, the relief; I was expecting dreadful news."

"Where can we go?" Ace stood close to her, breathing in the greasy-sweet smell of stage makeup.

She took him by the hand and led him down to a room behind the stage. By the low light of a tasselled lamp, Ace took in a mirrored wall, a table with a tea urn, a litter of upright chairs and a couch covered with a blanket. Without a word, they started to undress, flinging off each other's clothes until Elsie jumped naked into his arms, wrapping those golden legs around him. Ace hobbled them to the couch and thrust into her with a roar, and Elsie said, "Oh, my!" with her feet arching above them. They clung to each other in clammy desperation, and when the quivering turned to goose-pimpled shivers, Ace tucked the blanket round Elsie and climbed back into his dank uniform.

"Will you be alright?" he said.

Elsie nodded. "You'd best go now before Reg raises the alarm." She gave a shriek of laughter. "*Normally*, he's a really strict doorman."

Fire engines were racing along a parallel street when Ace emerged from the theatre. He set off at a run, and reached Dean Street to find the block of tenement flats near his grandparents had collapsed.

Zeidy and Bubbe were dead from the bomb blast. After identifying them for the record, he sat by the roadside weeping openly; he thought of their constancy in his life and the unbearable shrinking of the paternal link. Where was Kitty? Ace wanted her solidity as he hunched on the kerb. She'd be on a bombsite, reviving exhausted rescue workers with her steak and kidney pudding, still hot in the tin. Two more days and they'd be on their honeymoon in Torquay, just him and his stringent bride.

A wedding, a funeral, and four months later a telephone call.

"How did you know the number?" Ace stared at the newly installed phone.

"Oz gave it to me," said Elsie, and Ace held the receiver away from his ear to mute the intruding voice.

Kitty came up behind him and pressed her belly into the small of his back; phone calls were a novelty for them both.

"What can I do for you?" said Ace into the mouthpiece.

"I'm pregnant," said Elsie.

Ace had a coughing fit before he could carry on. "Congratulations," he said. "My wife's pregnant too." Kitty snuggled into him, circling his waist with her arms.

"Stuff your congratulations," said Elsie. "I need your help."

"What sort of help?" As he spoke, Kitty detached herself. Ace muffled the phone with his hand.

"A friend of Oz," he whispered. "She's in trouble." Kitty motioned him to talk to Elsie, who was shouting down the line.

"Sorry," said Ace. "I was explaining who you were to my wife."

"Were you now? Well, she'll understand then that you made me pregnant."

"No, that can't be true."

"It is true," said Elsie.

"How can you be so certain?"

"That's insulting, Ace. I haven't been with anyone else; that's why I'm certain. You're the only one."

The tremor in her voice vibrated in his ears, communicating a bilious sensation of ruin. He could not be responsible. He wouldn't allow anything to undermine his lovely marriage; it had to be perfect so Kitty would feel secure in *her* pregnancy. Elsie, he reasoned, was exaggerating her claim on him. She was, after all, a worldly Windmill Girl.

"Elsie," he said, " I'm sorry you're in trouble, but I can't help. The best thing you can do is talk to Oz; he'll know what to do."

Replacing the receiver, he turned to Kitty. "Did I do the right thing?"

She sat on an upright chair, arms crossed loosely over her stomach. "I wonder why you need to ask me that," she said.

"Because I've dumped her on Oz."

"And is Oz responsible?"

"Elsie thinks so."

"Then why did she call you?" Kitty's shrewd eyes were searching his face, willing him to make things right.

Ace stood before her, degraded and blaming Oz. It was he who'd persuaded Ace to go to the Windmill in the first place, he thought, so in a way, Oz *was* responsible. He knelt at Kitty's feet, burying his head in her warm lap.

"She's probably telling all his friends to strengthen her hold on him. He won't know if he's the father, but he'll help Elsie because he's a big-hearted bloke."

Kitty was silent. After a long pause she threaded her fingers through his coarse hair. Ace released his breath and shed a single private tear into the rough weave of her skirt. Had he got away with it?

PART TWO

CHAPTER NINETEEN

New Orleans 1960

Rose Tully sat on a stool at Woolworth's lunch counter, conscious of static in the air. As fellow students settled beside her, the restaurant manager approached.

"Four coffees and four doughnuts, please," she said. Her smile faltered as he loomed over her.

"You know the rule," he said, plucking the menu from her fingers. "I'll serve you, but not the negroes."

"We're asking you to serve us as regular customers," said Rose.

"And I'm asking you, all of you, to leave now. I want you out of here." He blew on a whistle as he walked away, and Rose glanced at her companions. It was her first sit-in.

"We stay," said Jackson. "Nice and easy. Make out you're studying."

Rose was taking a textbook from her bag when the lights snapped off and restaurant staff surrounded them. "We're closing." A lardy-pale man in a Woolworth's paper hat addressed the top of Rose's head while empty stools were carried away in the gloom.

"I advise you to vacate your seats or there'll be trouble."

Jackson nodded. "Heard you loud and clear," he said, and all four were still sitting when police arrived to arrest them.

"Yes, they were orderly, but they wouldn't leave," explained the manager. "I won't have them wrecking my business."

"Sir, we're backing you all the way." The officer in charge used a soothing tone. "The mayor and our chief won't tolerate demonstrations; sit-ins will not be permitted in this town." He fingered the billy club at his belt. " We'll be charging this bunch with criminal mischief."

Shoppers on Canal Street were lingering by the patrol car when the students were led out of the store, and a neatly-dressed woman holding a takeout cup moved forward and dashed hot coffee over Rose.

"Nigger lover," she said.

Before Rose was bundled into the wagon, she caught sight of frantic eyes in a face stretched with anger. She glanced at the dark stains splattered over her white T-shirt and knew this was just the beginning. She was nineteen, and her sympathy for the civil rights movement was leading her away from the comfort zone of debates and essays, into a frontline struggle.

Damn, she thought, and her bladder pressed for attention.

She'd grown up with liberal parents in the French Quarter, among a restless community of writers and musicians who moved for work between New York, San Francisco and New Orleans. Her father Leo was a photographer. Rose was fifteen when he came back from an assignment in Alabama with a smashed camera, and he'd let her sift through his black and white images. The early photographs showed 'Whites' and 'Colored' signs at a Greyhound bus station, and passengers sitting in their allotted seats: whites at the front, blacks at the back.

"All very neat and orderly," said Rose. "Just like here. How did the protest start?"

"With a woman in Montgomery who refused to give up her seat." Her father slid a portrait across his desk and Rose examined the calm face of a woman in spectacles with smooth centre-parted hair.

"She doesn't look like a troublemaker."

"The driver insisted she had to move, but she wouldn't, so he got off the bus and fetched a policeman."

"He arrested her?"

"Of course. She was violating the city's race laws."

"What did she say about that?"

"Rosa Parks said she was tired of being treated like a second class citizen."

"Did she?" Rose picked up the photograph, smarting with envy that this serene-faced woman had a clear cause to fight. The ache in her own life came from a baffling sense of loss, and she didn't know how to confront anything so nebulous.

"How did your camera get smashed?"

"It was madness. Snipers were shooting at the buses and I got in the way of someone lobbing rocks at the windows."

She leaned into his shoulder, a sour taste welling in her throat. She watched him leaf through the pile of pictures until he came to the close-up of a man with distorted features.

"Look at his face, Rose. What do you see?"

She shuddered. "He's snarling and scary – was he one of the snipers?"

"Yes, he's scary, but look at his eyes."

"Ugh, they're crazy!"

"Crazy with fear, maybe?"

"Fear of *what*? He's the one holding a rifle, isn't he?"

"Fear of losing the upper hand, I'd say."

Rose sat in her prison cell, embarrassed by the memory of herself at fifteen. Jackson had motivated her teenage angst and given purpose to being locked up for sixty days. He'd encouraged her and the other sit-in students to highlight their protest by making a public jail-no-bail pledge, and the judge reciprocated by giving them the maximum sentence. Leo Tully offered to post bond for his daughter, but Rose knew he backed her decision; he brought her a Carson McCullers novel to pass the time, and a Josh White album of blues songs to come home to.

She spent a lot of the time lying on a bunk that smelled of mice, mentally preparing herself for the next stage, when all-white state-sponsored schools were to be targeted. It seemed to her that shame underpinned the resistance to integration. The legacy of New Orleans' slave port past still lingered in uneasy spaces, and Rose wasn't alone in having a grandparent fathered by a colonial man's relationship with a slave.

Alerted by a scratchy sound, she rolled over in time to glimpse the twitch of a cockroach scuttling under the bed. Her skin shrank against the grime-stiff blanket covering the mattress, and she sighed at her own weediness. She'd heard of isolated prisoners befriending a bug, but she wasn't lonely. And looking at the whiteness of her thin, goose-pimpled arms, Rose knew her confinement would be tolerable. Unlike Jackson, she hadn't been made to strip naked on the first day and walk the humiliating length of a corridor. And while she gobbled up a lunch plate of well-cooked black-eyed peas and pork gristle, she knew the burnt food she'd smelt would have gone to the black cells.

She saw Jackson once a week when she was taken for a three-minute cold shower. That was her outing, and he was usually at his door, ready to deliver a news bulletin through the bars.

"Three arrested at McCrory's dime store," he murmured as she walked past. "Charged with criminal trespass."

If the guard was distracted, Rose lingered in the passage drying her hair with a skimpy towel while Jackson gave her struggle guidance. She watched his hands describe the limp-response technique. He had the fingers of a musician, she decided, before finding out he was an engineering student from Mississippi. Rose didn't know him well, but at the meeting in a church to rally support for the lunch counter sit-ins, she'd scrutinised the way he magnetised people with his eloquence. And once they leaned towards his soft-spoken words, Jackson's velvet voice erupted.

"This is a pivotal moment in history! Together we can dramatise the abuses of discrimination and advance the struggle for equality."

Rose was aware of solidarity building in the church.

"There'll be resistance and arrests, but our butts will be on those stools. Jim Crow laws are unconstitutional, but they won't be abandoned unless we insist; *nothing* will change without our civil disobedience."

Rose held her breath as Jackson's gaze swept over her before taking in the whole room.

"Who's willing to join the frontline?"

All hands went up, and Rose thought how clever he was to make a lunch counter protest sound vital and cool to students ripe for jumping on buses as freedom riders. For herself, Rose didn't know if she had the muscle for a violent backlash to peaceful protests, but in memory of her Creole grandmother, she was prepared to explore the territory.

She got out of jail in time for Ruby's first day at an all-white school. Leo was covering the event for *Life* magazine and Rose walked with him through the rundown streets of Ninth Ward, feeling judged by grim faces.

"Everyone looks so sullen." She moved closer to him.

"This downtown white neighbourhood's been hand-picked by the school board," said Leo. "You're looking at people who already feel powerless. They're afraid of an invasion of black kids in their schools."

Rose looked away from hostile stares. " This integration test is going to fail in a spectacular way."

"Damn right. Our local leaders have thrown all their resources at resisting change. They even passed a law to close Louisiana's public schools if a single one was threatened with integration."

"Threatened..." repeated Rose, as they reached the elementary school on North Galvez Street. She took a sweatband from her wrist and bundled her ochre hair into a tight knot as chanting women marched towards them.

"Stick with me," said Leo. "Here comes little Ruby."

Rose looked up to see the six-year-old first-grader approaching the front steps of the school with an escort of federal marshals. The women stood aside in a jeering group, and as Ruby drew level, one of them spat on the child's slight shoulder.

"That's a disgusting thing to do!"

Rose surprised herself by shouting, and almost ducked as the woman swung round, a bubble of saliva still clinging to her lower lip. She braced herself for a thump when the woman raised a forceful arm, but it was only to wipe her mouth on a coat sleeve before speaking.

"A race-mixer, are you? Well let me tell you what's disgusting, you crab fat yellow Communist. The burr-heads ain't got NO place in our school. I won't have my children infected with the Dee-segregation."

Rose backed away from the toxic words and walked into Leo, crouched low behind a camera. She moved to steady him, but he was already springing forward to focus on Ruby climbing the school steps, trailed by a television crew and several news reporters. She watched the solemn girl disappear into the building, and moments later, hundreds of white children erupted through the double doors and swarmed down the steps with their cheering mothers. Rose picked up a bag of her father's equipment, hugging it tightly as she imagined Ruby witnessing the scene.

Over the next few days of accelerating violence, Rose vacillated. Her mother Alice joined volunteers to make a safe corridor for three black girls enrolled at another downtown school, and Rose saw that her commitment was wholehearted. She wanted to be like Alice, but she wasn't. She held back, uncertain of her footing. That was how she thought of her reluctance, and the queer little phrase bugged her. She flexed her toes to clear her mind and walked over to a small group at the school gates, where she met the few white parents who still brought their children to class.

"Every day you're being subjected to abuse and stone-throwing, but you don't give up." Rose tried to sound like Jackson, and she raised her voice as mounted police came into view. "Your brave and important stand for human rights is an inspiration to others."

She knew it was much worse for black parents. Ruby's father had lost his job, and when she learned from a mother in the crowd that the child's grandparents had been evicted from their farm, Rose found her footing and pushed through a threatening mob in search of Jackson. She found him laughing with journalists.

"The mayor blames *you* for all the trouble," he was telling them. "He says the presence of a large press corps is disruptive: you're not supporting the supremacists in your coverage."

He turned to Rose. "You look hot! What's fired you up?"

"I want to know who's responsible for running Ruby's family off their land."

"I can tell you that." The newsman in a squashed trilby stepped forward and tipped his hat to Rose. "I'm writing a piece for the *New York Times*. The White Citizens Council of New Orleans is behind it. They're like an uptown Klan: no physical violence, but a speciality in economic reprisal. Evicting the kid's grandparents from the farm where they've lived and worked as sharecroppers for a quarter of a century is just their style."

Rose looked at the dents in the journalist's much-travelled hat. "I'm glad you're writing about it," she said. "What shall *I* do, Jackson?"

"Best thing is what you are doing: support for the white parents still hanging in there. The Citizens have organised a hate-campaign against them; they're being ostracised at work and bombarded with abusive calls at home. We don't want the parents to back off."

Rose watched the journalist scribble in his notebook. Jackson was probably right, but she wanted to be closer to the drama of Ruby's family. There was a cramping sensation in her sneakered feet until Jackson fished a Freedom Now button from his pocket and pinned it to her jacket. He laid a brotherly hand on her shoulder, and Rose looked into his iridescent eyes.

"Okay," she said, and walked jauntily back to the picket line.

Chapter Twenty

It never occurred to Rose as a child to question the colour of her grandmother's prematurely seamed skin. She was just Mawmaw, who made her a patchwork quilt with the cotton wool she'd picked on the plantation. Rose wouldn't be parted from it. Her mother had to spread the quilt over her at night in such a way that the soft edge touched her nose. Stroking it with a finger released a drowsy scent of wood smoke, and Rose would slide the fragrant cloth against a nostril and drift into an easy sleep. Mawmaw grew sick and died when Rose was four, and she took to wrapping herself inside the comforter. She dragged it round the courtyard, making up stories under the magnolia tree that featured a magic cloak; sometimes it flew her to see Mawmaw. It gathered leaves and mud, and late one night her mother sneaked it off the bed, sponged it clean and hung it out to dry. Rose was found next morning standing under the clothes line, nose against a damp hem. But the sleep-inducing smell had gone forever, and the magic with it. The faded quilt fell from favour and Rose forgot what Mawmaw looked like.

She was a dreamy child who thrived on the itinerant household of her parents and their mobile friends. If Leo and Alice were busy, there was always someone to talk to, someone with a funny name. 'Pops' showed her his photographs of French Quarter architecture, houses like the one she lived in. She recognised the crooked wooden shutters, the squiggly patterns of iron balconies and the peeling blue doors. Webby was a poet who introduced her to words like 'elliptical' and tried to teach her chess, and Funky Joe called her Blossom and allowed her to watch him practising *Freight Train Blues* on his cornet.

"Why am I Blossom?" she asked one day.

"Your skin," said Funky Joe. "You is cream like a magnolia blossom."

She stared at his dark face and remembered Mawmaw.

"Should I be black?" The five-year-old was frowning at her pale hands.

"No 'should' about it," said Joe. "Your grandmammy was black, your mom be the colour of honey, and you is blossom-white. That's the way it mixes."

Rose was puzzled but Funky Joe was already blasting away on his old cornet.

When they all pulled chairs to the table that night to share a pot of jambalaya, Rose looked from one face to another.

"Why are we different colours?"

Webby cackled wheezily. "I'll tell ya. Joe here comes from Africa, where skin is black to shield it from the glaring sun; Pops is brown 'cause he's from the Caribbean where the sun ain't so fierce, and I'm kinda gray on account of the light a day not reaching me in a regular way."

He started coughing so Leo took up the theme. "I'm bleach-white because I come from the chilly North; your mom has gold skin because she's precious, and you, Rose, are cloud-white because you were born in London when bombs were falling from the sky.

It was like a fairytale to Rose. She looked round the table at the indulgent adults, and all that mattered at that moment was feeding her hunger. She sniffed at spicy whiffs of okra sauce as her mother ladled out plates of shrimp and smoked sausage with rice.

"Bless this food," she gabbled, and nearly choked on her first mouthful, tickled by imagining she was a hungry cloud.

About this time, Rose invented a family companion whose gender was optional. Oak was a strong boy when she offered his help in carrying Leo's camera bags, and a nimble-fingered girl when Rose put her forward to weave the cloth Alice hadn't time to finish. Both parents agreed their loads were lightened by the unseen intervention, and Alice explained it as 'fairy magic'.

"Shush!" Rose clamped her hand over her mother's mouth. "Oak is *real*."

Alice lifted Rose's hand from her face and rubbed at the ink-stained fingers. "Well, at least tell me what Oak looks like."

"How can I tell you that?" Rose's voice was a scandalised whisper. "No-one knows."

She'd invented this androgynous personality to take her place when she was busy. Rose had started drawing with a fine-nibbed pen, and once a composition gripped her she didn't respond to anyone. Oak was her surrogate; a pliable entity alert to the pileup of domestic chores, and always available. Oak was her filter, who most likely wore rubber boots and a swirly skirt like Rose, with an old hat of Leo's that slipped over the eyes.

Her drawings were funny or dark. She had a tendency to exaggerate facial features so that portraits loomed into caricatures, and landscapes with luminous detail would develop into starkly scratched places inhabited by gaunt creatures. Alice said they were haunting, which encouraged Rose to show her latest picture.

"What is it?" said Alice.

Rose contemplated the formless mass positioned above a sharp surface of jagged edges. "It's the shape of a shadow," she said.

It was Funky Joe who gave Rose a feeling for the blues. She was twelve when he came back from performing with a three-piece band in New York, all fired up by the political songs they'd been playing.

"White folks *appreciated* our music," he told her, shaking his head.

"Course they do," said Rose. "When I hear you playing your cornet it gives me the shivers."

She watched him rub liniment over his dry lips and zip the instrument into a bag. "Where are you going? I want to go with you. Please let me hear you play."

Funky Joe shrugged his bony shoulders and she followed him to a coffee shop near the river. It was the club where Webby sometimes read his poems when musicians and folk singers had vacated the tiny stage. Funky Joe bought Rose a wide cup of hot chocolate and sat her by a table of chess players while he hopped onstage to perform. He'd hooked up with an acoustic guitarist who announced he would sing Josh White compositions. Rose had no idea what he meant by saying they were from an album of Jim Crow Blues, but she joined in when the random audience hollered approval.

The music was mellow, the lyrics obscure, and Rose lifted the cup to her mouth with both hands, inevitably binding the taste of chocolate to the sound of the bitter-sweet blues. She was tapping her foot to *Uncle Sam Says* when one of the chess players looked up and shouted "Cops!"

Two officers were blocking the doorway.

Rose stared at their bulk and sat listening to the owner explaining his business to the Law.

"That is correct," he was saying. "I do not have an alcohol licence because I do not serve liquor."

Rose became aware that the club was emptying through the back door and a hand was grabbing her arm. Funky Joe yanked her from the chair.

"Get yourself outta here! You dreaming?"

She looked into eyes blurred with panic. "What is it?"

"I'm responsible for you and I don't want to be arrested."

"Why would they arrest you?" Rose shrank from his pitying expression.

Funky Joe took her hand gently and led her to the exit. "Listen

Blossom," he said, when they were close to home. "When you grown a bit more you'll understand all manner of things. You will come to know the ways of crazy-ass white crackers; you will make it your business to know."

Rose knew she was privileged. She knew her grandmother had died aged forty-five, 'worn out by slavery' her mother had said, and most likely abused by some crazy-ass white cracker. She repeated the phrase to herself in Funky Joe's sleepy voice, and tipping back the brim of her hat, she saw that she already reached his shoulder.

"I am grown," she said.

Chapter Twenty-One

1961

Twelve months on the frontline changed Rose. For one thing, her hair stood on end. Its texture once resembled the tassels of a maize cob, but each strand of hair had now coarsened into a stiff upstanding bush. Her nose changed too, convincing Rose that her streaming nostrils burned from inhaling the sharp stink of hate.

She sat in the library, holding a tissue to her face in the reading room. She was scanning copies of *Times-Picayune* for its coverage of the schools boycott, muttering at the paper for being so reactionary. Here was a group calling themselves Knights of White Christians, and they'd been given a whole page to publicise their beliefs. Rose read the headline, Black Plague Stalks the Land, and let her head sink to the table.

"May I help you?"

Rose eyed the librarian. "I don't believe so."

At twenty, Rose still miscalculated people. Her own ambiguous sense of self made her flounder; she had no idea if this woman wanted to help. In college, her lurching attempts to be sociable puzzled arts students on her course. "I'm sexually ambivalent," she'd said conversationally to the boy who sat next to her in the canteen, and he said, "Really?" before turning to talk to someone else. "I'm socially inept," she told the girl who asked for the loan of a pen, and the only response was, "Oh". Small talk eluded her.

"Please, tell me what's troubling you." The librarian's voice was kind.

"I'm ashamed of my race." Rose rested her head on scarred wood and saw inked words scratched into the surface.

"Oh my, that *is* a burden."

Rose sat up and looked into her bleached blue eyes. "You understand?"

"We have members here who wouldn't tolerate reading a book returned by a black person. 'Germs' they say. And they're supposed to be educated."

Rose had an urge to let her head slide back to the table and relieve her spindly neck of its throbbing weight. "I feel useless," she said.

"Come with me." The librarian's low tone was insistent, and Rose followed her in a bovine trudge, eyes fixed on the sensible shoes leading her into an office.

"Now we don't have to keep our voices down." She settled them in chairs and extended a hand with pearl-polished nails. " I'm Colette Peck. I've seen you at the school barricade, haven't I?"

Rose lowered her head to obscure gathering tears. "I tried to help a family, but they've been driven away."

Colette Peck poured cups of long-brewed coffee and handed one to Rose.

"I can see you're quite tuckered out," she said.

"I'm mad." Coffee slopped in Rose's saucer. "I thought I could help but it's hopeless."

"No, not hopeless. When I take books to the school I try to block out the venom and concentrate on that little girl, Ruby. She's been there for one year now, having individual tuition with a dedicated teacher – isn't that remarkable?"

"It's pathetic," said Rose. "I'm sorry Miss Peck, but she's still kept separate from the other girls. Is that the best we can do?"

She tried to hold back a press of unwelcome images, but they kept on coming. She was dimly aware of a handkerchief being pressed into her hands as she gave way. She wept until she felt desiccated. Miss Peck sat with her, deflecting staff inquiries until Rose mopped her face and volunteered to launder the sodden cloth.

"Oh my, it contains a breeched levee of tears," said Miss Peck.

Rose nearly managed a smile. She pushed herself upright and made for the door. "Something caught my attention," she said, before going back to the reading room to look at the defaced table.

"How predictable." Her voice, echoing round the room, elicited darting looks of disturbance from readers sitting near the WHITES ONLY message etched in wood.

Miss Peck was in the science section when Rose went to say goodbye.

"Here it is," she said, moving a long fingernail down the index of a medical journal. 'Tear-gas poisoning'. I believe you're suffering from the effects of a crowd control agent."

Rose wondered why she hadn't thought of it herself. It was more acceptable to have symptoms related to an irritating chemical anyway; more tangible than a reaction to hate.

"I need a break from crowds," she said. " I need more music in my life."

Rose started frequenting a new jazz café in the neighbourhood. The weathered old building had once been an art gallery that encouraged jam sessions, and when the new owners saw her doing quick sketches of the musicians, they invited Rose to hang them on the wall. She established herself at a corner table with her pot of Indian ink and a variety of pens, and hours passed while she worked on her illustration of a tuba player, lips vibrating at the cupped mouthpiece, buzzing sounds through sixteen feet of brass tubing. Drawings of Funky Joe were fluent and sure: in a few strokes, she implied his jutting bones and brooding eyebrows, and the layers of her spiky-textured scumbling indicated the nervy state of his energy.

She wanted to draw a new sax player in town, and while she waited for him to turn up for a gig at the café, Rose sketched a picture of her grandmother from a fading photograph belonging to her mother. She used a brown pigment to echo the sepia tone, and her pen caressed the tight-scrolled ears she didn't remember.

"You is a fine artist," said Funky Joe, leaning over her shoulder. "Those are her eyes, exact."

Rose glanced up. "You knew her?"

"Her and my grandmammy were friends when I was a youngun." He stared at the likeness and nodded. "They made pralines to sell, and I scraped the bowl."

Rose stippled an area with tiny dots and sat back to see the perspective. "I think I've inherited her eyes."

Joe gave out a rolling chuckle. "Ain't possible, Blossom, when you is not blood kin."

Chapter Twenty-Two

Rose planted herself in the doorway, trying to still her wild breathing. Alice, at home weaving, peered at her through a loom of indigo threads.

"You been running?" She was working on one of her bed covers, and she paused only to motion her daughter to sit.

Rose dragged a stool across the polished floor and sat on the edge of it. She used to like the hypnotic rhythm of Alice at the loom, interweaving her layers of yarn into cloth and working geometric patterns into the deep blue wool. Balanced now on the stool, her jaw tightened as the insistent shuttle shifted between threads, and the Weft and Warp words she'd learned as a child set up a repetitive rattle in her brain. Alice sat straight-backed and focused; Rose hunched in a jangling fog.

"Why didn't you tell me?"

"Help me with this, Rose; the yarn's tangling."

Rose simmered on the stool. "Did you ever plan on telling me?"

Alice's head jerked up from her work. "What are you talking about? Where's your father? Never around when you..."

"Are you my mother?"

That stopped her.

"I've been your Mom since you were three months old." Alice's voice was calm, deliberate.

"You never told *me*. You and Dad never ever said *any*thing. How could you leave me to find out from Joe?"

At the café, Rose had sat very still, pen mid-stipple, a brown dot seeping through the paper, spreading into a dark and shapeless blob.

She'd stared at the bulge of Funky Joe's stricken eyes until he blinked. He seemed to be having trouble speaking. She shook his arm. "*What* did you say?"

"I never meant..." His voice ebbed away.

"*What?*

Joe hung his head and mumbled. "It's a wretched thing I done."

Alice was talking. "Leo and I..."

" How could you do this to me?"

"Rose, listen. We wanted you to know, but when we adopted you there was a condition. We agreed to say nothing about your birth. That was the deal. We wanted you so badly."

"What about me? Did I badly want to be parted from my own mother?" Rose rushed at Alice, and the loom collapsed under their joint weight.

"Holy mackerel!" Leo stood in the doorway pulling his hands out of a film-changing bag.

Rose wrenched herself free from the wreckage and retreated to a corner of the living room, glowering at Leo as he released Alice from a web of yarn.

"What the hell's going on?" He looked from his wife's shaken body to his daughter's eyes, skewering him with contempt.

"You tell *me*," said Rose. "Explain to me why I've been deceived for twenty years; why you've lied to me all this time about being my mom and dad." Her voice cracked. "Who am I?"

"Sweetheart!" He tried to hold her but she shrugged him off.

"Leo," said Alice, "we owe her the full story."

Rose sat on a cane rocker in the corner. She crossed her arms tightly round her ribs and faced them with a mask of relentless endurance. "I'm waiting."

Leo joined Alice on a couch by the French windows. "It began in London," he said.

Rose pitched forward in the rocker. "I'm *English?*" She cradled her head in her hands. "Why were you even allowed to take me out of the country?"

"There was a war on. London was a dangerous place to be and..."

"Was I an orphan?" This was a scenario she could deal with; she could reconstruct them as heroes, rescuing a baby from the blitz.

"No," said Leo.

Rose rocked herself in the chair like an abandoned child.

"Your mother was very young," said Alice. "Her parents wouldn't let her keep you."

"How young? Where was my father?" The rocker ground against bare boards.

"Elsie was just eighteen, and not married. She never told her parents who he was. Leo's the only father you've known."

"Elsie." The rocking stopped. "Tell me everything you know about her."

"There isn't much," said Leo.

Watching his pained face as he described where Elsie had lived, Rose imagined a thin person with a big belly stepping cautiously over the rubble of a bombed city. He mentioned a wrecked place called Stepney with narrow streets, and a hospital called St Peter's where Elsie gave birth. Her parents, he said, took it badly.

"In those days," said Leo, "the Brits referred to illegitimacy as a dreadful slur on family respectability. She had no say in the matter. They took you away from her."

"Leo, Rose wants to know about her mother." Alice stood up, and catching sight of her ruined loom, sat down again. "It's true that Elsie's parents took charge, but she made the condition we agreed to. Elsie couldn't bear the idea of her baby growing up with the knowledge that she'd been given away by her natural mother. She was thinking of you."

"That's so weak." Rose picked at a piece of interwoven cane until a strand worked loose on the chair arm. She jabbed a finger in the hole to widen it. "It's obvious she just wanted rid of me."

"No, my darling." Alice sprang from the couch and sat on the floor by the rocker, taking Rose's rigid hands in her own. "She was younger than you are now, stripped of her rights. She was forbidden to meet us, though she managed it for a few minutes when we went to collect you at the hospital. She wanted to know who was taking her baby. The staff said she had no business being there – no business! Poor little thing."

Rose pulled her hands away, and the cane she'd been picking at snapped off in her fingers with a sharp crack. "*I* was the poor little thing, not that whore."

"Rose!" said Leo. "She was a dancer at a West End theatre. We weren't entitled to know anything about your background, but she did tell us something. She said your father was a fireman. That's all we know."

Chapter Twenty-Three

Jackson knew all about displacement. "Never have known who my real folks were," he told Rose when she spilled her news. "It was my aunties who put me through school; they watch over me. Long as you have people who care about your life Rose, you are *way* ahead."

She'd fled to the downtown Baptist church on Carondelet where Jackson ran non-violence workshops.

"I feel like a phoney," she said.

Jackson gave her a piercing look. "Explain yourself."

"I thought I had a coloured grandmother, but I don't."

"You sure about that?" Jackson laughed. "Where does your powerful hair come from?"

"Jackson, I'm *English*."

"You telling me British people aren't mixed? Listen Rose, you can drop out anytime you want. Just be clear about your reasons."

"I'm not clear about anything."

"So your pedigree is white as your skin implies; does that invalidate you as an activist? Hell no, it makes your position solid. You don't need Creole roots as back up."

He glanced at the clock on the wall. "Time for the group. You helping me?" He lunged at her, swinging an imaginary billy club, and she went limp and rolled away effortlessly across the floor.

"Flawless," he said. "Stay with us Rose. I'm one of the people who cares about your life."

"You're reeling me in like you always do." Her look was reproachful, but gratitude spread like arnica over her bruised heart.

Long before the end of the session, resolute volunteers were clamouring to be freedom riders on the cross-country bus demos. Jackson was discussing the philosophical roots of civil disobedience when a wiry youth with troubled skin leapt to his feet.

"Don't confront me with this shit, man." He backed away towards the door. "I can see where all this is heading, and I'm not going to ride no Greyhound and get the shit beat outta me by them Ku Kluxers. I'm gone!" The door slammed and the room shivered into silence.

Cross-legged on the floor, Rose contemplated Jackson's unruffled features, and anticipated his straightforward response. He was one of the few people she trusted.

"His point of view is valid," said Jackson. "Make no mistake, it's gonna be a bumpy ride."

Rose didn't care. A bumpy ride would be the antidote to her fractured state. She was looking for trouble. Her mother – adoptive, for god's sake – worried about her being beaten up, but Rose was a fireman's daughter. She hunched over, cramped by a knot of confusion. Leo was her dad; she loved him, admired him. How did he find her in London?

"Pay attention Rose. You coming to Washington with us?" Jackson's thatched eyebrows had bunched together.

"F'sure I am. When are we going?"

"Spring break, next Monday."

"Count me in." She stood up. "I have to go."

"We haven't finished."

"I'll *be* there Jackson." She picked up her bag. "I've got a heritage thing to deal with."

She found Leo in his office by the darkroom with his hand on the telephone. He swivelled in his chair as she walked in.

"Rose. Good," he said. "I've rented a vehicle for next week. If you and your CORE friends want a ride to Washington, I'll have the space."

"Why are *you* going?"

"You know why. It's a *Life* assignment."

"What were you doing in London?"

"When? Oh, I see." He leaned back and knuckled his eyes. Rose knew they must be tired from hours of printing.

" I was taking pictures for *Life* even then, but mostly freelancing for *Picture Post*. I walked the streets of Stepney recording The East End at War – that's when I heard about you."

She stood over him, bristling. "What! What did you hear?"

"Back off Rose. This isn't an inquisition." Leo rubbed his cratered face and sniffed his fingers. "Developing fluid," he said.

"You're prevaricating."

"Quit looming over me and I'll tell you."

Rose sat on the desk and let her legs thud against the side.

"Listen to me," said Leo. "I've never regretted what we did; we found a delicate war baby in need of a home, and we offered her one."

"Dad! That's the end of the story."

"I'll always be your dad, you know."

"What if I find the fireman?"

"Then you'll have two."

"Would you mind?"

"Yep. I'd probably want to kill him for letting you go."

"So you did meet him."

"No, he was just a detail. I had the impression that the young mother – your mum Elsie – got very little support from anyone close to her. Her parents were dire."

"What was she like?"

"Intimidated; a bundle of anxieties. She wasn't supposed to be there for the handover, so I guess it showed strength of character that she was determined to meet us. Alice was so upset. It was supposed to be a happy event for us, but it made her feel like a baby-snatcher."

"She was – you were. You snatched me away from my life."

"Rose, you're being dramatic. We went through the adoption process." He pulled open a drawer and took out a pack of cigarettes. As he lit one and inhaled, Rose said, "You don't smoke."

"I do in a crisis." Leo leaned back in his chair and shut his eyes.

"Give me one then. I'm in crisis too." She slid off the desk, poked a cigarette in her mouth and fumbled with the lighter. She studied a family photograph on the wall while she smoked: they were on a paddle steamer, all three windblown and standing close together. She looked about three years old, squinting into the sun with ribbons in her hair and a fluffy cardigan over a pale frock. Leo, she thought, had the lazy smile and wavy hair of a matinee idol, and Alice looked like a carefree beauty with her billowing curls and peep-toe shoes.

"Why didn't she have her own baby?"

"Your mom?" Leo ground out the half-smoked cigarette and examined the grey ash. "She couldn't."

Rose leaned closer to the picture, absorbing the face of a barren beauty. "She always told me I was the only child she wanted."

"She was telling you the truth."

Rose spun round as though the word was barbed. "Why should I believe you?"

"Oh Rose!" Leo sent the chair in a swivel as he clambered out to give her stiff body a hug. "No reason," he said, letting her go. "Truth is an ephemeral thing at the best of times."

He slumped back in the chair and appeared to be talking to himself. "It was her work with the Kindertransport that made her want to adopt. Alice used to meet them off the train at Liverpool Street Station. They had numbered labels round their necks, and she matched up each child with their luggage and linked them up with their sponsors or foster families. They all had places to go, and she'd come home to me feeling empty."

Rose watched Leo, the witness of turbulent times, revisit his past. She wanted to return the hug, but she didn't. She quietly left the house and took the St Charles trolley back to Jackson, who knew all about displacement from the inside.

Chapter Twenty-Four

1965

Riding on the back of a flatbed truck with her camera focused on leaders of the march, Rose came to the conclusion that Jackson was a shrewd operator.

"Learn to live like an orphan," was his obscure response when she tried to burrow into his private space three years earlier. She'd run into his arms intending a wild and passionate liason with her magnetic mentor, but she hadn't bargained for Jackson being a righteous man.

"I'd be taking advantage of you," he said, arms hanging passive. "You're in a precarious state."

"I always suspected you were pretentious." Rose lashed out in humiliation and was bundled off to Frenchmen Street to register new voters.

Each time she clung with limpet urgency, he peeled her away and nudged her into another project of numbing worthiness; didn't he realise she was in love with him? She only admitted it to herself in weak moments: Jackson was her prime motive for being an activist. She dared not tell anyone, imagining accusations of flippancy from classmates, and worse from fellow campaigners. She retreated into a steely space, and was operating like an automaton when Leo offered her a Leica and some master-classes.

The camera gave her a sense of identity, and here she was, crouched among journalists and photographers in the back of the truck, feeling legitimate. These were her comrades: professionals reporting the struggle, free of messy emotions.

Leo had flown off to Africa with Alice to photograph wildlife. He was ground down, he said, by the taste of tear-gas, so Rose edged into the gap, a darting shadowy figure who only once got black paint sprayed over her precision lenses. Freelancing for a photo agency, she had one picture published around the world of an elderly woman being jet-hosed to her knees. It gave her accredited access to press areas, and singled her out for jostling by the sheriff she snapped in Selma.

"You goddamn magazine photographers!" he bellowed, shoving her aside. "My advice to you is to get out of town. And if you ignore my advice, lady, I don't care if they stomp the hell out of you."

Rose skipped away with her graphic portrait of a man with rattlesnake eyes.

At dawn on the third day of the march, the truck was bouncing towards Montgomery while Rose braced herself against the tailgate and tucked her unbrushed hair into a turban of Kente cloth. She kneeled on her bedroll, still damp from the field she'd slept in, to photograph marchers coming over the hill as the sun rose. In the wide-angle lens she saw them as silhouettes, six-abreast with arms linked, their singing voices obliterated by the overhead clatter of helicopters.

"What's the song?" She shouted to Matt, the newsman beside her.

"At a guess, *We Shall Overcome*." He grinned at her. "I like your headpiece."

"You'll like this, too." She was focusing on a one-legged man among the walkers. "Did you know an amputee was marching?"

"He's come the whole way – fifty four miles."

Rose liked a journalist who did his job; Matt had already borrowed a motor scooter to trail up and down the length of the marching column, and now he was jumping off the ambling truck to pick up one of the leaflets being dropped from a small plane.

"An unemployed agitator ceases to agitate," he read, when he was hauled back over the side. "No bite in that message."

Winding new film into the camera, Rose could tell Matt was watching her. "What?"

"Nothing. You're dedicated, aren't you?"

It was a novelty not to be taken for granted. Jackson had demanded total commitment, and in her infatuation she'd moulded herself to his expectations and lost her sense of humour. She breathed out and expelled a significant weight. She thought her skin would split from the rare smile stretching the curves of her face, and she touched the softness of her mouth with curious fingers.

When she looked up, Rose noticed the rough stubble and scattered freckles on Matt's face, and responded to the candour in his watchful eyes.

They made a good team, Rose and Matt, covering major news events together, and they were a couple even before they left Montgomery. The defining moment, they decided, was the night they shared a tent on cow pasture; they were eating peaches on the grass when the farmer stopped by to question their politics.

"You're nothing but unwashed trash," he said in response to their liberal views, and walked away. Then he turned and stood looking at them in their blue jeans and sweatshirts, his mouth stretching into an unpleasant sneer before the parting shot: "You're dressed worse than the scarecrows on my farm."

They dived into the tent, burying their faces in bedding to muffle the gales of laughter.

"How come it's so easy being with you?" Rose was puzzled that he could spontaneously rent a shabby studio apartment in the French Quarter just to be near her.

"I'm a simple sort of dude and I'm bowled over by your bushy-haired boldness. I've never met such a well-defined nut."

"You're not simple, Matt – you're bloated with cheek."

"I don't have issues; not primal ones. I spring from uncomplicated Philadelphia stock, whereas you, my warrior queen, are in foundling territory, scrambling for roots."

She relaxed in his clasp of empathy and loved him for wanting to help find her birth mother.

"We'll start with the hospital where you were born." Matt was already flipping through his address book. "I'll ask colleagues in London to do a trace, and if anything positive comes up, we'll take a trip and do our own detective work."

She considered the possibility of finding Elsie. "Suppose I hate her?"

Matt put his arms around her. "You might, to begin with. Do you want to take the risk?"

With her face tucked into his neck, Rose pictured childhood memories fashioned from stories Leo told her at bedtime. He'd lulled her to sleep with tales of the Peaceful People from Ireland. They were his potato-eating forbears, the Tullys, who'd braved the epic sea voyage to America to escape famine. Images of adventuring relatives in salt-stiffened tweed would slide across her eyelids until she drifted off to the roll of her father's voice.

But she wasn't a Tully. She pulled away from Matt. "I have to find out, even if she is an old toad."

"It's *medieval*." Matt was sitting in the main square with Rose, eating a breakfast of beignets and coffee while they went through their mail. He was reading a letter from his journalist friend John, who wrote that children adopted in England weren't entitled to information about their natural mothers.

"The official records are classified." Matt's eyes widened as he scanned the contents. "He says they're sealed to protect mothers who want to remain anonymous." He swallowed mouthfuls of sweet fritter and signalled for a coffee refill. "I don't believe it."

'Why not?"

"I've been checking news clippings from the period, and the attitude towards unmarried mothers was vindictive. Babies were taken away and offered to foreigners."

"Get rid of the little bastards," said Rose.

"America's gain." He leaned over the table and gave her a passionate kiss.

She knew he wanted her to feel secure, but her dismal origins were giving her vertigo.

"I don't want to go on with this, Matt. What's the point? England's a miserable place."

"Listen to this. John says he thinks the law will change because there's pressure from thousands of people like you. They're campaigning for a mutual-consent registry."

"Bastards united. That's neat."

Three days later, Matt was commissioned by a news agency to cover Vietnam.

"Why now?" She tried to keep the panic from her voice. "Hundreds of reporters are there already."

"The war's escalating; anyway, I want to go." He held her bleak face in his hands. "It won't be for long, darling Rose. We've got the rest of our lives together."

He sounded like a soldier taking leave of his sweetheart, and the words clogged like corn in her throat.

He was gone by December and Rose played music to mute the ominous drumming in her head. Charlie Parker's penetrating sax worked the best; she put on *Cool Bird* five times before Funky Joe burst into the room and said, "I got an idea."

The intimate apartment she shared with Matt was dark without him, and she'd moved back to the wide-windowed family house for the company of stray visitors. Leo and Alice were still in Africa photographing wildebeest, but Joe and a few other musicians were back in town.

"Me and Coochie Pete is playing with The Café band tonight; if you is blue, Blossom, this be the music for you." Joe tugged at the recent goatee tufting his chin. "We are *sharp.*"

"I'll think about it," said Rose.

"No sense thinking about it. Pete's made gumbo and it's time to eat. Then you put on yo party hat and shimmy by to hear us play."

She followed him to the kitchen where powerful smells of okra-thickened stew rose from the pot Pete was stirring. His goggle eyes and fleshy lips brought a deep-seabed fish to mind, but his smile was pure dolphin as he scooped steamed rice into bowls.

"Hey ma'am, I hear yo belly *growling.*" Coochie Pete wheezed with laughter and heaped her plate with chicken and peppers.

Sitting at the scrubbed pine table, Rose opened its deep drawer to find cutlery and came across the lace mats crocheted by her grandmother. She smoothed them with a remembering hand and looked over at Funky Joe, his greying head bent towards the food; she was glad the ease between them had been restored. Coochie Pete passed round cans of beer and urged them to eat, accompanying the meal with repeated finger riffs pattered on the table edge.

Rose sighed. "There was music in that gumbo." She gathered the dishes and took them to the sink. "What time are you playing?"

"'Bout ten," said Joe.

"Okay if I bring my camera?"

"Ma'am..."

"Pete, call me Rose, or Blossom."

"Well, RoseBlossom, pictures of the band would be mighty helpful. We doin' a big tour soon..."

"And there's cash in the pot for publicity," said Joe.

Rose glimpsed a shift in her focus. She saw how the world of music could absorb her; how she could use her camera to document the circumscribed lives of black musicians. She tried it out on Joe and Pete.

"Circumscribed you say?" Pete shook his woolly head. "My vocabulary don't run to a genteel word like that. An uppity niggrah like myself would choose a word with more flavour."

Funky Joe cackled. "Something like 'stunted'?"

"F'sure has flavour, but I had in mind a *juicy* word like emasculated."

Funky Joe jumped out of his chair and hopped about. "Never would associate such a word with you, Coochieman. Lighten up Blossom; we is honoured if you take pictures, but don't go heavy on us. Put the word *celebrate* in yo brain and let the music take you there. No struggle shit, you hear?"

Chapter Twenty-Five

London, 1966

A bouncer known as Midnight nodded them into the club. Rose and the band settled themselves at a table and tucked into steak and chips after their late night set round the corner at Flamingo. Rose forked mushy peas into her mouth and shut her eyes, tasting London on her tongue.

Funky Joe reckoned her moody black and white portraits of New Orleans musicians helped the band secure a series of gigs in the English capital. He'd simply added 'Photographer RoseBlossom' to the support crew list and said, "You comin'."

"Try stopping me," said Rose. Easy as that. The music was taking her there.

On the flight, she'd started doodling in the margins of a newspaper. She made caricatures of the glamorous airline staff while they eased their way through the cabin dispensing their incredible smiles. And as she sketched, her imaginary childhood pal Oak hopped unbidden into her mind, offering to help find her fireman dad. Rose stuffed the paper back into the seat pocket, rattled by the juvenile intrusion. She sat on her hands to make the figment fade, but it had already stirred up possibilities and she turned to Joe in the seat beside her.

"Did you ever hear anything said about my real father?"

Joe was preoccupied by the high-heeled perfection of a hostess stalking by.

"What you askin'?"

"If you know anything about my biological dad."

Joe stared, and the words came slowly. "Only daddy you got is my friend Leo. One special human being. Why would ya want another one?"

"Because there is another one."

"I know you is adult Blossom, but consider the pain of finding a man who desires to be unknown to you."

The private sorrow in his eyes reminded her: no struggle shit, he'd said.

Most of the bluesmen Rose knew came from fractured backgrounds. They led precarious, buzzy lives; their hearts were large, their ways bizarre. They shaped all the elements into song, shared their rhythms with anyone who cared to listen, and dazzled her with the imperishable glow of their art. Photographing them while they played their instruments, she tracked the knots that shifted about their faces and tried to capture the visceral moment when the stuff of life streamed into the music.

A DJ played twelve-bar blues, and couples wiggled to *The Hucklebuck* while Rose finished her late night meal. When she pushed the plate away, a whisky and coke was placed in front of her.

"From Mick, who admires the hat," said the waiter, indicating a skinny man in a coat of velvet patches.

Rose was amused that her mismatched clothes and taste in men's hats had reached a stage of being cool. She raised the glass, but the thin man was swinging through the exit door.

"Looks like a treble," said Coochie Pete, noting her drink as he rose from the table.

"Who's the man leaving?"

"That dude is mighty appreciative of our music. Sang Delta blues early on. He be the Rolling Stones' singer."

“Wow!” Rose wanted to run after him, but it clearly wasn’t his intention. She drank the whisky instead and danced the night away in her remarkable hat.

They emerged from the basement to the cheery racket of Soho’s dawn street cleaners. In Wellington boots and waterproofs, burly men hosed and scrubbed the mucky gutters, singing lewd refrains and lobbing jokes and the odd jet of water at each other. Rose and the band stood rooted to the pavement until the boisterous spectacle moved down the street and turned a corner.

“I have to lay down my head.” Funky Joe sagged against the club wall, whimpering. “I forget where we sleeping. Where’s our manager?”

Rose hooked her arm in his and he crumpled against her. “Find me a pillow Blossom, and I’ll help you find an English daddy.”

They’d been given a flat to use above the recording studio two streets away. Rose led the way, with Joe flopping beside her and the rest ambling along behind. Her landmark was a pub called The Crooked Toad; three doors along from it was an insignificant door that opened into a gloomy hallway smelling of mould. Tiny mushrooms sprouted from the skirting boards, and the carpet sank with a squish underfoot as they climbed two flights of undulating stairs to their beds.

Earlier in the day, they’d unpacked their bags and examined the flat.

“Man, this place has not been loved for a long time.” Coochie Pete slid his finger behind a bulging ornamental panel and withdrew it at speed. “*Bugs.*”

“English folk ain’t too concerned with hygiene, I surmise.” Funky Joe was in the bathroom, awed by the heavy mineral stain crusting the bath from a leaky tap. He cracked with laughter when Pete came to look.

"Where's the rest of the tub?" He bent to find the tap end tucked into an alcove that extended through to the kitchen.

"Ingenious use of space." Joe swivelled on the spot. "And see how this curtain opens to reveal the john?"

Pete's frogeyes bulged with dismay. "That is not ingenious; that's unsanitary. That is not a place to take a dump with impunity."

Rose opened the door to a six-bed room where the band had dropped their belongings. "Here's your pillow Joe."

She heard a snore before she turned the handle to her own single room. She tiptoed over creaking floorboards to the window, and as she looked at the red telephone box in the silent street below, a woman stepped out of it wearing a tiny silver skirt and long boots. Rose watched her loiter for a minute against the box until a man approached, and without a word, she turned abruptly and set off on tapping heels with the man in tow.

Rose slipped off her clothes and sank into bed, longing to hear Matt's laconic voice, craving for his lean body. The sheets weren't fresh, but she burrowed into them with only one thought: tell Matt about Mick Jagger. That would bring him home.

Chapter Twenty-Six

The lopsided man who met the band at the studio introduced himself as arts historian Stevie Weavie. He was recording the music of legendary bluesmen, he said, and wanted to include Funky Joe and Coochie Pete in his archive of American giants.

Joe and Pete were both in their late thirties; they'd grown up playing music. Over the years they travelled back and forth across America with different groups, recorded twelve-track albums with bands in Chicago, and formed the well-respected Blues Four Quartet with a pianist and a drummer. But in all that time they'd never been honoured as giants.

"We is *legends*?" said Joe.

"I've been following your careers." Stevie lurched about on stunted legs, animated by their presence. He described Joe's cornet-playing as 'inspired', and referred to the 'genius' of Pete on guitar.

"I also sing," said Joe, as a matter of fact.

"I've heard you." The historian's loose shoulder-length curls shook at the memory. "Your gravelly voice is unmistakable. The tone's sublime."

Rose lifted her camera and recorded the fleeting majesty of Joe's expression. Here was a man accepting recognition as his due. It gave his face a stature she hadn't seen before, and she had caught the moment. The surprising pinch of envy that followed was a revelation to Rose: she wanted to be a legend.

Stevie led them through to the control room, where cardboard egg boxes were visibly glued to the ceiling.

"Good old-fashioned sound treatment." Ned, the recording engineer, had followed their gaze, and the musicians fell into each other with squawks of mirth; they weren't prepared for quaint British detail in a studio equipped with the latest multi-track tape recorders and high fidelity headphones.

Under Stevie's meticulous direction, the afternoon session dragged for Rose, and after using several rolls of film on the Blues Four, she crept away to get some fresh air. She emerged from the stuffy basement to find the narrow Soho street humming with exuberant young men. They were strolling by in sharp suits and shined shoes, walking around each other talking, voices speedy and lyrical. For a moment, they swept her along with them.

"Like your style," said the one in winklepicker shoes, and because they were wearing trilbies much like her own, Rose asked if she could take a picture.

"Yuh know we are Jamaican ska dancers," said Winklepicker, stating a fact.

They formed a tight group and struck poses like professionals against the street's façade of 17th century terracing. Rose finished the film in her camera with seven arty shots while she told them what she was doing in London. At the mention of the Flamingo Club, Winklepicker leapfrogged over a bollard.

"That's where we dancin to the rhythms! At the blue beat sound session. Yuh heard Al Capone? Ska-Lip-Soul? Prince Buster, he is dah *emperor.*"

They swarmed off down the street in a cheeky chatter, calling back, "Walk good, American." Rose stood in the road until they were out of sight, buzzing with their energy and a premonition that music would lead her to a dancer called Elsie.

Walking back to the studio, she passed a music shop where a reflection among the guitars in the window seized her attention. The scarecrow image in the shiny glass was familiar; wiry curls sprang from under the hat, and the loose clothes and baseball boots accentuated bone-thin legs. It was an androgynous look based on comfort, with plenty of pockets for lenses and spare film. Rose didn't often look in full-length mirrors, and she peered at herself now with a curious eye. At twenty-five, she didn't look like anyone she knew.

In The Crooked Toad, with pints of beer in hand, Stevie told the band why he was lopsided.

"Polio as a child," he said. "I'm telling you so you don't have to speculate. I hate people speculating about me."

Joe fingered froth from his whiskers. "Suppose you wish us to confide 'bout our own selves. You is welcome to speculate, Weavie man."

"On your raunchy nicknames?" Stevie polished his wire-framed glasses as though to sharpen his wits. "I associate yours with the *Funky Butt* song; sending dancers into a sweat with your demon cornet and..."

"Whole room packed with them stinky bodies belly-rubbing." Joe's eyes glazed with memory. "All drinking whiskey, and me not more than a boy, stirring them with *Buddy Bolden's Blues*." He drained his beer glass and belched luxuriously. "You going to tell your story, Pete?"

"Damned if I will. This man here may feel obliged to explain why he crippled, but my sexual proclivities are my own business."

"No need to be so touchy." Stevie stood up and moved towards the bar as Rose bounced into the pub, elated after a long-distance call with Matt. She'd been cut off before there was a chance to brag about Mick Jagger, she said, but Matt was alive in Saigon, travelling with a US combat unit and filing dispatches. She pulled over a bar stool and rattled on about London fire stations until their unnatural silence intruded.

"What? Am I interrupting something?"

"The historian is leaving," said Pete.

"Must dash, but I look forward to your photos." Stevie put a fresh round of drinks on the table, shook her hand and limped away.

The whites of Pete's bulgy eyes flared. "Faggot!" His savage whisper travelled like a missile towards the departing figure.

"Something I missed?" Rose looked enquiringly at Joe.

"He made a pass at Pete. Imagine that." His voice was stern but his mouth dimpled.

"Twisted in body, twisted in mind." Pete glared at Joe. "You wouldn't be sniggering if it was your nuts being fumbled." He picked up his guitar and made for the door. "Later," he said, and was gone.

Drinkers around them returned to their own conversations and Funky Joe bought a Martini for Rose and several packets of salty pork scratchings. He crunched his way through all her questions, and when the packets were empty, he brushed crumbs from his goatee and sat back.

"Thing of it is, Blossom, Pete will not be persuaded into that studio again whether we be finished or not. My feeling is he was mistaken, but he a proud man and there's no changing what he thinks. Now you was talking 'bout fire stations, but I didn't get the drift."

"Something Matt mentioned. That I could start checking records for London firemen in the war."

"You have some identification?"

"That's the problem." She lifted the cocktail stick out of her glass and nibbled on the speared olive.

"You expecting me to come up with something? Blossom, you is fishing in a empty pond." He sat forward with a start. "Fish. They were gutting fish."

Rose watched Joe's forehead buckle with effort. "*Tell me.*"

"The grandmammies. They were talking 'bout the mystery of your whereabouts; yo origins."

A lively group pushed through the door and jostled past their table to the bar. Rose could see Joe's lips moving, but the words didn't reach her.

"WHAT ARE YOU SAYING?"

Joe snapped back to the present and took a long draught of beer. "Only thing I recall is he had a surprising name. Something short, like Bud."

"Bud?"

"No, *not* Bud. Something like it."

She started laughing uncontrollably, imagining herself calling on every fire department in London to locate a man with a three-letter name. And if she ever found him, why would he be pleased to acknowledge a stork-legged girl in a man's hat as his daughter?

Funky Joe smiled broadly. "Guess they mixed you a powerful cocktail, Blossom."

Chapter Twenty-Seven

New Orleans, Spring 1975

It started with Jimi Hendrix. Rose photographed the bluesrock guitarist at his first London gig, rings on his fingers, afro hair beneath a tall hat. She took close-ups of his large hands and the thumb he used to fret bass notes, and as he became famous, so did the name RoseBlossom, attached to the portraits in gritty black and white that defined the psychedelic era and magnified the musician's short life.

"Why don't you use colour?" Reporting the war for a decade had left Matt hungry for bright images.

"Colour's distracting." She was looking through a pocket lens at the contact sheet of a Grateful Dead concert. "Look at the luscious tones."

"I want distraction." When he didn't take the magnifying glass she offered, Rose hunched over the proofs again, marking the images she was going to print.

"I want a divorce."

Looking at a fuzzy picture of Garcia, she said, "You want a horse?"

"I want your attention!"

"Matt, you know I have a deadline. *Rolling Stone*..."

"Fuck the magazine. I want a divorce."

She hadn't misheard at all.

In situations of stress, her instinct was to become invisible. Expression drained from her face and her body took on a stillness that amounted to absence. In this state, she strained to make sense of the hazard: Matt wanting a divorce after nine years together.

They'd got married after his first assignment in Vietnam; a gorgeous Mardi Gras wedding. The guests wore spangled costumes, parading flamboyantly through the streets to a masked ball after the nuptials. They sang the carnival anthem *If Ever I Cease to Love* with its nonsense words, Rose and Matt whispering to each other, "May the fish get legs, and the cows lay eggs, if ever I cease to love – *you.*" They danced nose to nose in their sequinned masks, marvelling at the fit of his squashy nostrils with her fluted ones. And when he tripped over her trailing lace skirts and stripped her to the waist, he gathered her into his arms, covered her body with kisses, rushed for the exit. He didn't stop running until they reached home, where the honeymoon began to the accompaniment of a brass band trumpeting by.

Their new home had a neglected lemon tree in the courtyard and room for a couple of chairs and a table the size of Matt's typewriter. He sat in the shade writing articles for the *New York Times*; she nurtured the tree, and over time it flowered and drenched the space with a sweet hypnotic scent. They ate meals out there, read books to each other, made love on a rug laid over the cracked flags. The season changed and Matt was drawn back to Vietnam, back to colleagues covering battles from the trenches. His reports began to reflect a growing opposition to the war, but he couldn't keep away.

"I know you think it's macho bullshit," he said, assembling his kit for one more trip. "Your world of music has its place, but 'Nam's the story."

"Listen, you patronising hack, 'my' world of music is part of the story. There were half a million kids at Woodstock, demonstrating peace." She picked up a tube of mosquito repellant from his luggage pile and read the label before tossing it back. "You were in a jungle when I was in the field listening to Hendrix. His version of *The Star-Spangled Banner* was 'seminal'."

"I didn't need to be there. I can listen to the record."

"It's the anthem for the anti-war movement now."

Matt had stopped packing. She remembered the liquid look in his eyes sparking her desire as he scooped her up and carried her to bed. Her belief in the power of music made her an irresistible hot patootie, he said. How lucky, she thought, that her lover was the guy she'd married; a sexy man of courage and passion.

She didn't recognise him when he came back from the seventh trip. He shambled through the door, brushed past her and flopped on the bed without a word. When their little son Josh rushed in and swooped on his Pops, Matt buried him in his arms with dry sobbing gulps. He growled at Rose when she tried to extricate Josh, so she lay beside them both, talking about the conjuror he'd missed at their son's fifth birthday.

"Talk to me," she said, when Josh had wriggled free of his father to fetch his box of magic tricks. She felt the clamminess of his hands, but it was days before he mentioned the land mine. Leo and Alice advised patience, but Rose was waking in the night, and Josh was wetting the bed. She cajoled and prodded her inert husband until he released enough fragments to piece together.

The colleague he was working with had stepped on a mine. Matt saw the journalist and a combat photographer being blown to pieces. He wrote his story in the military aircraft carrying American dead from the jungle to Saigon, knowing two of the green plastic body bags held his friends. He dispatched his article and went to a bar. He'd been drinking ever since.

She extracted the details from him while he consumed a bottle of Bourbon, crouched in an armchair staring at footage of his country pulling out of the war. He watched TV all day. Or he watched her.

And now he wanted a divorce.

"The fish have grown legs?" Rose turned on Matt with challenging eyes.

"I don't understand."

"*Think about it.*"

"Rose, I'm so tired."

"You need medication. Do you want a divorce, or a doctor?"

"You know I've found a lump?"

"What sort of a lump?"

"In my groin."

Rose was willing to be sidetracked. She had no experience of men falling to pieces. Leo had changed direction under stress, exchanging the wild behaviour of Southern extremists for the wildlife of Africa. And Jackson, after witnessing assassinations and holding a murdered friend in his arms, had flown to Washington as a lobbyist.

"I'll make an appointment for you with Doctor Bloom," she said.

He was watching TV with the volume off. "Do as you like," said Matt.

There was no divorce, but she was losing him. The anti-depressants induced twelve-hour sleeps and disorientated him for the rest of the day. When she came home buoyant from a photo shoot at the Warehouse on Tchoupitoulas, she collected their letters from the mailbox and flung open windows to air the apartment. She put on Isaac Hayes to maintain her mood, and as the *Theme from Shaft* began to build, she went to sit beside Matt in front of the silent screen. He gave her a vacant smile when she offered him a handful of letters, but he didn't take them.

"They're yours," she said. "You ought to look at them."

"Where's Josh? I want to see my boy."

"He's with Alice and Leo, learning how wildebeest mark their territory. Open your mail, Matt; it's piling up."

"He's interested?"

"He's fascinated by the size of their dung heaps; Leo told him they shit copiously." She put the letters on his lap and saw his legs stiffen.

"You deal with them. I – can't." His strangled voice was pitiful to her, but when Rose leaned over to give him a hug, he shrank away.

"Matt, what's to be done? I don't know you."

"Open the damn letters and leave me alone."

She snatched up the pile and took them into the office, where the record was ending. She changed it for Hayes' *Hot Buttered Soul*, wishing she'd photographed the aesthetic dome of the singer's shaved head on the album cover. Reluctantly, she moved to the desk and sat down to sort the mail. The writing on the envelopes began to blur, and several teardrops plopped on an aerogramme, diluting the ink and dissolving the words Matthew Shepherd.

Her husband's name, fading before her swimming eyes. It spooked her, thinking of his personality disappearing.

The letter was postmarked London, and the sender's name was unforgettable. When she first saw the byline John Death in *The Times*, Rose had remarked on the name. Matt said people saddled with the synonym often added an apostrophe and pronounced it De Ath, but his English friend John revelled in the original. He even wore a black cape to enhance his surname. Rose had never met him, but she liked the sound of this eccentric journalist; she opened his letter expecting a wacky feature idea for Matt to follow up.

Hackney – May 17 1975

Congratulations, Mate. I hear your personal Fall of Saigon story from the belly of a Hercules is up for a press award. A finely-balanced piece of reporting, if I say so with envy, and remarkable under the circumstances. I went to Wally's funeral in Wiltshire, and his family were immensely touched by your intimate portrait of him as a war correspondent. It was read out at the service – not a dry eye in the church. We'll miss the old rogue.

Now for something completely different. Remembering you once asked me about tracing your wife's English biological mother, I thought you'd be interested to know that only a decade later, it's possible. Adoptees' birth records have been unsealed now the danger of misuse has passed. Don't ask me what that means, it's island mentality paranoia, but the good news is that a mutual-consent registry is being set up to help connect people.

I've already taken the liberty of checking the October-December 1941 records from the Stepney hospital where your wife was born, and found that seven babies were adopted in that period. Would you like me to investigate further, or can I persuade you to come to London to do the search? It's time you crossed the pond again, and high time you introduced me to your family.

Affectionate Regards,

John

Rose took the flimsy blue letter to her husband.

"I never saw your last dispatch, Matt. It would have helped."

"It might have helped *you*, but it finished me off." He kept his eyes on the TV.

"Dr Bloom says it's post traumatic stress."

"Soldiers get that, not civilians. Not a dickhead gonzo." He waved her away and turned up the volume.

"Read the letter." She shouted through a wall of sound. "Some people think you're a hero."

Back in the office, Isaac Hayes was singing *By The Time I Get To Phoenix*. Would that be her story? By the time she got to London, her natural mother would be gone? She put on a pair of sneakers and went to join Josh at his grandparents.

She found him sitting on the floor of their photographic library, surrounded by Leo's discarded pictures of elephants. They were all close-ups: the corrugated skin of a cheek, the bristly flap of an ear, a soft-lashed eye, an enormous foot. He was using them like jigsaw pieces to make a whole animal, while Alice was filing colour transparencies. If Alice was hurt by her adopted daughter saying she wanted to find her birth mother, she masked it skilfully, thought Rose. She scrutinised her calm smiling face and saw only signs of encouragement.

"Of course you need to find her, darling. You're thirty-four and a mother yourself; it's a good time to look for your roots." Alice sat on the floor beside her grandson to help with the elephant jigsaw. "Go to London with Matt and leave Josh with us."

Rose was about to tell Alice she was irreplaceable as her mother when the phone rang. A magazine wanted wildlife photographs. She watched the lithe way Alice rose from the floor and carried the phone towards the relevant files, gathering details from the picture editor. The mother I love, thought Rose.

Chapter Twenty-Eight

1975

From the moment Josh screamed, Rose dreaded the trip to London.

"Don't leave me behind. Something bad will happen." His stuttering sobs had been uncharacteristic, heart-rending.

"It's natural," said Alice. "He's never been parted from you." She crouched before her grandson. "It was just an idea, Josh. I thought Grandpops and I could take you to see real African elephants while your mom was away."

Rose saw he was tempted; he pulled on his loose-lobed ears before deciding.

"I have to stay with Pops. He's not well, you see. I'm the one who makes him better."

"How do you do that, Doctor Josh?" said Alice.

"I tell him a story. Of course it has to be a good story – maybe about a alligator with broken teeth. I can tell him any story I like and there has to be a made-up word in it and Pops has to guess which one is it."

Alice was hooked. "Can you give me an example, Mister Word Inventor?"

Josh shook his head and Rose explained. "The words come out of the story, don't they. What about the cabbage fish? That was a good one."

"Yes! A fisherman catches one in the river and he thinks he's got a veg'able. That's mighty strange, he says to himself. It looks like a cabbage and it smells like a cabbage so he throws it in the water and the fish swims away, safe for another day."

Going over those days when she was making plans for the three of them to stay in London with Matt's friend, that odd Josh phrase bounced into her mind. Other details remained obscure; Rose couldn't remember Alice saying anything about going to Texas. There'd been talk of Africa, but obviously she hadn't been paying enough attention. She'd been fretting about the consequence of finding Elsie Slater.

Elsie Slater. Her birth mother's name. John the journalist had followed the trail and come up with an address in Stepney for the Slater family. The rest was up to Rose.

They left Louisiana during the hurricane season. She'd already checked the long-term weather forecast and no major storms were predicted for New Orleans, but she asked Matt: "Can a person be affected by atmospheric electricity?"

He managed the hint of a smile at her thick hair seething with static charge. "You look wired," he said.

John met them at the airport in a top hat and pink leather boots. He towered above the crowd, his deep voice booming across the arrivals hall: "Matthew Shepherd!"

Josh was thrilled. "He's a giant in lady boots."

John gravely shook his hand. "Small person," he said, "do not be deceived by the pinkness of my footwear. I am a manly man." He turned to charm Rose while Josh discovered an English coin in the palm of his hand.

With an arm around Matt's sagging shoulders, John led them to the decommissioned taxi he'd bought and drove them to his home in Hackney. "I'm in the process of restoring it," he said, when they looked up at the tall cracked building. "Bomb-damaged old houses are going cheap in grotty parts of London, and you and I, Matt my old mate, are going to patch it up and turn it into a palace."

A vision of Victorian splendour snared Matt's imagination and, with trowel in hand, his limp shoulders began to lift. Rose had no interest in the plastering job offered; she took Josh on sightseeing trips while she considered how to approach the Slaters of Stepney. She had a telephone number, but she couldn't bring herself to make the call. She kept finding a puppet show or a circus they must go to, and another week slipped by.

"Think of yourself as a doorstep journalist," said John. He was up a ladder, grouting. "Go to Popham Street and knock on the door. Confront them." He climbed down to her level. "You're afraid to phone in case they won't see you. Take the train to Stepney Green. Do it."

That was all she needed.

The bell was a chiming one, and she was still listening to its hallway echo when the door opened and a woman in hoop earrings said "Yes?"

"Hi. I'm looking for Elsie Slater."

The woman's broad body blocked the doorway. "You're American."

"I was raised there, yes. Does Elsie Slater live here?"

"Who's asking?"

"Haven't I said? My name is Rose Shepherd. I'm – related to her."

"We don't have American relations in our family."

"I was born in London."

"Were you now. Well, I don't know what business you have coming here, but I've got to get the dinner on so you'd better spit it out."

"I'm her daughter."

"*Flipping Ada*." The woman turned and bellowed down the hall, "Mum!" Over her shoulder, she said "You'd better come in. Shocked me rigid, you have."

“Are you…?” began Rose, as she hurried to catch up.

In a living room stuffed with furniture, Mum was rolling up pop socks over her veined legs. “Hang on a tick,” she said. “Not dressed for company.”

Rose apologised. “I should have phoned to say I was coming.”

“But you didn’t because we’d have said don’t bother.”

Rose sat down uninvited. “It’s hard for all of us, but I wanted to meet my mother – just once.”

“Don’t look at me with your big doe eyes,” said the woman with ear hoops. “I’m Margaret. Elsie was my sister.”

“Was?”

“She died years ago. Cancer.”

“Make a pot of tea, Marge. Our visitor looks peaky.”

While her daughter was in the kitchen, Mum Slater made it plain to Rose that she wasn’t a curious person. “We had you adopted ducks, and that was that. Elsie got on with her life.”

“Are there photos? I’d love to see them.” Discouraged by the silence, Rose tried again. “Do I look anything like her?”

Mum Slater’s bullet-grey eyes surveyed her. “No, can’t say you do. Now where’s that tea? Marge!”

On the tube back to Hackney, she didn’t immediately recognise her reflection in the window. She’d dressed simply for the occasion in jeans and denim jacket, tying down her restless hair with ribbons and pins to appear unthreatening. She poked out her tongue at the neat image in the glass before dragging the restraints from her curls.

“I could have had a burlap sack over my head for all the interest they showed.” Rose talked between mouthfuls, eating with her fingers from a roasting pan of John’s speciality sweet and sour ribs.

“You were the murky past on their doorstep.” John dished out rice to his guests at the kitchen table. “You reminded them of buried history.”

Rose examined a neatly stripped bone on her plate. "They didn't want to know *anything* about me."

Matt leaned close. "If Elsie'd been alive, it would have been different."

"They didn't want to talk about her; they wouldn't even show me pictures."

"They were never going to accept you, darling. Me and Josh, we're your family."

"Exactly so." John poured wine. "Let's be thankful the Slaters of Stepney didn't deposit you in a Barnardo orphanage."

Rose drained her glass. "I never thought of that." She went to check on her sleeping son while John made custard to go with his baked apples. She came back as he was dishing up.

"Josh has an old grey rabbit in his arms."

"My childhood favourite," said John. "In exchange for helping me core the apples."

"You're full of surprises. Were you an only child?"

"Tell me you love the taste of English custard, and then I want to hear the rest of your story – I detect that the visit wasn't a complete waste of time."

"You're a wonderful host and a shit-hot sleuth, but the yellow sauce sucks."

John refilled their glasses. "Here's to plain speaking. What *did* you find out?

"Nothing about Elsie, but the name of a man who was a friend of hers and the wicked fireman."

"That was cheeky, asking about her boyfriend."

"I didn't. They were trying to get rid of me."

"And the man?"

"A cab driver called Oswald Bagley. Known as Oz."

Rose started packing, edgy for home. Josh had school, she had work;

they'd been away long enough. Matt stopped painting the bedroom wall to watch her.

"What about the Oz connection? Aren't you curious?"

"Why am I chasing after people who don't give a damn about my existence? It feels wrong."

"Give me a couple more days to finish this room, then we'll go."

The news next day led with the bombing of the Hilton Hotel in Park Lane. If John had owned a television set, Matt would have been watching every news programme; instead he devoured the batch of papers delivered daily and listened to all the radio bulletins. He made regular announcements himself.

"The *Daily Mail* received a ten-minute warning of detonation – not long enough for Scotland Yard to evacuate the building, so they said."

He rustled his way through several versions of the story. "The bomb exploded in the hotel lobby, killing two guests and injuring sixty two. One man lost his legs. The glass frontage was blown out and people in the street were knocked to the ground by the blast.

"Now here's a neat detail: diamond necklaces and precious stones fell among the wreckage of the hotel jewellery shop."

He paused to listen to the radio muttering in his ear. "The BBC says the IRA's claimed responsibility and London is on a state of high alert. Several areas of the capital have been sealed off after a series of hoax warnings following the blast."

Rose looked up from labelling canisters of film. "I don't want to hear anymore."

"Don't you want to know that the Supremes are staying at the Hilton?"

"*Stop*. What else is happening in the world?"

"There's a story from Washington about President Ford escaping an assassination attempt by a woman with a pistol."

"You're kidding." Rose looked at the front page he held up. "What happened?"

"She was wrestled to the ground by a presidential bodyguard."

On an inside page, Matt spotted a small news item – just a paragraph – about a heavy storm in Texas surging through Port Arthur and uprooting trees in Beaumont. He didn't mention it.

Rose was defensive when a police officer visited her nearly two months after their return. He was asking her to visit a morgue to see if she could identify three bodies found after the hurricane in Beaumont.

"I don't understand," she said. "I don't have family in Texas."

"Where are your parents at this time?"

"Somewhere in Africa. They were planning to photograph elephants."

"Have you heard from them?"

"No, but that's not unusual when they're on safari."

"Is it usual for them to be away this long?"

"Yes it is. Why has it taken the police eight weeks to find people who died in the storm?"

"Ma'am, there was no systematic sweep of houses on the assumption that most people had relatives looking out for them."

He wouldn't leave until she promised to locate her parents and inform him at the police department. After he'd gone, she fastened on to the memory of Alice offering to take Josh to see African elephants with Leo. That's where they had to be, somewhere south of the Sahara Desert, following a migration path where keeping in touch was impossible. Letters from them were rare anyway, and Leo often didn't call her when he was away because his ethic was to focus entirely on the job in hand.

"It's not unusual," said Rose out loud. She listened to herself, knowing Alice would have wanted to hear about Elsie Slater. She would have found a way to call.

"Why do the police think they've found Leo and Alice?" Matt was back with Josh from school, making a stiff drink for Rose and himself.

Her face was vacant. "I don't know."

He took her chilled hands in his. "Did you ask?"

"What's wrong with me that I don't know where they are? What sort of daughter am I?"

"You're the sort of daughter who accepts her parents' eccentric ways. Now let's be systematic about this: you search their house for clues and I'll phone the police to establish what they know. Take Josh with you; he's good at finding stuff."

"Did you know," said Josh, as they walked along St Peter, "that elephants use their trunks like noses? They smell water that's twelve miles away."

Matt was right: Josh knew where to look for the captioned photographs of a trip to Chad, though it was 1974 when they'd followed savanna elephants through the dry season. He also found Leo's current desk diary. Rose sped through the abbreviated entries for August and September, stopping at a list of hire car companies beside a scribbled name with a Texas phone number. How dare they, she thought, pulling the desk phone towards her and dialling the number. She was listening to the disconnected signal when Josh brought her a notepad. He'd found it propped up on the light box in the picture library.

ROSE

Friday 6am

Darling Girl, we're about to set off for Beaumont on a mercy mission to collect Leo's godmother Tilly. She's persuaded him to rescue her from being put in an institution after making a "scandalous" public display of herself. Lord knows what we're letting ourselves in for, but we'll soon find out! I'm so keen to know if you've met your birth mother. Such a momentous journey for you. Whatever happens, you are my precious Rose.

Affectionately

Alice

Josh tugged at her arm. "Mom, where are they?"

As a journalist, Matt extracted all he needed to know in two phone calls. Officer Wishbone emphasised the powerful winds that characterised the Texas hurricane, explaining in some detail their destructive nature as they tore through Port Arthur to the heavily wooded neighbourhoods of Beaumont. Ancient oaks were uprooted, he said, and falling trees accounted for the extensive damage to buildings.

A blue clapboard house crushed beneath a mighty pine was only one of many.

"Our priority, Sir, was the safety of evacuees. Many were trapped on a gridlocked highway, and the heat in those cars reached 98 degrees. People were dying."

"I understand," said Matt. "And in the days, in the *weeks* that followed, I expect your focus was on accounting for all the residents who didn't manage to evacuate."

"You will appreciate, Mr Shepherd, that during the storm small boats from the Department of Wildlife and Fisheries were used to rescue people trapped in their homes."

"That's good to know. Now, what can you tell me about the three occupants of the blue house you referred to? How did you identify them?"

Officer Wishbone consulted his colleagues in Beaumont and adopted a sympathetic tone when he called back. "Mr Shepherd, Sir, the elderly lady of the three, Mrs Lilian Spruce, was the known owner of the property. We found travel documents suggesting the other two may be Mr and Mrs Leo Tully, but we still need positive identification. That's why we visited your wife. I'm sorry for the anguish."

"If it had been my in-laws, they would've evacuated her and…"

"Mr Shepherd, if it's any consolation, the couple died instantly; impact of the tree."

"And the old lady?"

"She drowned."

"Drowned in her own home?"

"It happens, Mr Shepherd."

PART THREE

CHAPTER TWENTY-NINE

Soho, London September 2002

Ace looked up from his empty glass as a familiar figure shuffled through the doorway of the Tavern.

"Oz, you old bugger, I thought you must be dead."

"Didn't stir your bones to find out, did you?" Oz gave a hacking cough before settling himself on the bench beside Ace. "Flu nearly snuffed me out, but I'm hanging on for showtime."

Ace calculated that if he was eighty-eight, his old pal was in his nineties and entitled to wander in his thoughts. He studied the battered old face, the still-shrewd eyes, the tufts of coarse hair springing from his nostrils.

"You're a survivor, like this place." He gestured to the barman and two pints were brought to their table. "What brings you here?"

"Showtime, like I said. Your past is about to catch up wiv you, me old diamond, and I want a ringside seat." He drank deeply and wiped his mouth on a spotted handkerchief. "You don't know what I'm on about, do you?"

A queasy sensation slithered into the pit of Ace's stomach as his memory regurgitated scraps from a shameful event. It was the only time Oz had come close to thumping him, and the only time Ace would have welcomed being beaten to a pulp just to ease the guilt. But all that was at least sixty years ago.

"You'll have to fill me in, Oz. I'm in the dark."

"With pleasure, old chum." Ace watched him rummage through his pockets and knew that whatever Oz produced, the impact would derail him. He braced himself against the smooth oak back of the bench as Oz held out a creased letter addressed to Oswald Bagley.

"Want to see for yourself, or shall I read it to you?"

"My eyes are bad," said Ace.

"You look sick as a dog." Oz gave him a sympathetic nudge. "It's not that bad, squire. Your American daughter wants to meet you. She wants to get to know you before it's too late."

"Too late?"

"Before you croak."

Ace wished himself dead at that moment. He was too old for a confrontation of such magnitude.

Long ago, he'd written a couple of songs alluding to the legacy of denial, but his enforced confession to Oz had released only a bitterness towards his father for the cowardly gene he'd inherited.

Though he tried as a young man to avoid territory where he might put others at risk, he'd come a cropper with Elsie. That's how Oz put it when Ace admitted his hour of passion with her.

"It only happened once," he heard himself plead, before Oz came at him with bulging eyes and bunched fists. He bowed his head to accept a beating.

Oz dropped his arms and stretched his fingers. "You're pathetic." He said no more, but he'd allowed Ace's wife Kitty to believe Elsie was his own responsibility, and he supported Elsie financially when pregnancy interrupted her career as a dancer.

Remembering this big-hearted response, Ace grabbed Oz by the arm. "Before I croak, let me tell you something. You've been the most remarkable friend to me. You protected me from disgrace and saved my marriage…"

"There's a big 'but' coming."

"What?"

"You'll chunter on a bit before telling me you're too gutless to meet your own daughter."

Ace huddled in his coat, considering the corrosive effect of his behaviour on family life. In the early days, Kitty had trusted him; she'd willed him to be the inspiring man she married. Their first daughter Lily was born while they were still in love, and Ace composed a jazz ballad for sax of such ineffable sweetness that its impact on even the sternest tear ducts became known in the trade as a Lily Gusher.

By the birth of their second daughter, Ace was having an affair with a fan of his music. He kept it secret, his justification to himself being Kitty's disinterest with sex during an arduous pregnancy. The affair ended within a month when Kitty clambered over him in bed one night and said "Wake up, Ace, I'm about to ravish you." Darling Kitty, who reclaimed all his attention until the next pregnancy. He didn't want her to be pregnant again; two children were enough. He resented her swelling belly and diminishing lust, and blamed Kitty when he slid out of control again. He couldn't explain the spectre of fear evoked by dependents.

"Harsh but true," he said to Oz in the pub. "I'm spineless when it comes to offspring. My daughters hate me."

"They only hate you because of the way you treated their mother."

"Exactly."

Oz patted his arm. "All this is bollocks. They're tough with you because you're a grouchbag. The unknown daughter doesn't know that. She doesn't know nuffink about you."

"She knows one thing. I knew one thing about my father."

They both concentrated on finishing their pints before Ace spoke again.

"Forget it Oz. This meeting isn't going to happen."

Chapter Thirty

Hackney, London 2002

Rose eased her suitcase through the doorway, levered off her boots, and flopped to a floor-level bed. After climbing four flights of stairs, it was a bonus finding a soft spot to land in John the journalist's top room. She propped herself against big Afghan cushions and pulled a foot towards her to massage pinched toes. Her eyes travelled over walls of autumn-leaf colours, shelves of books up to the ceiling, and a long table with television, computer and telephone among stacks of newspapers, magazines and neat towers of small change.

"Make yourself at home," he'd said as he was leaving. She arrived from New Orleans as John was setting off for Washington, unexpectedly assigned to cover 'War on Terror' talks at Camp David. She was to sleep in his room because the house was full; his sister and family from Ireland had stayed on to meet her. "They'll show you where everything is."

At the front door, he'd pulled on a rumpled linen jacket and kissed her cheek. "You don't need a boot up the bum this time, do you?"

Rose gave him an amiable shove. "Get going, smartass."

"Where will you meet?"

"At his local bar in Soho."

"In public – that's good. Take the 38 bus to Old Compton Street."

In his room, she braced herself against the rugged cushions, recalling the last visit to John's house; the grimmest year of her life. She'd only got through it with the distraction of a second pregnancy. Leo Junior, she calculated, must have been conceived in this very house, when Matt emerged from zombieland to reclaim her. Twenty-six years ago. And now young Leo was in the Marines.

"Why do you want to join a fighting force?" He was packing for boot camp while she was preparing for London.

"They've started a brilliant martial arts programme. Me and my buddies, we've signed up as reserves; not the real thing."

"But you could be drafted."

"Nah! We get the same training, but we won't be full-on Marines. Haven't you heard of Weekend Warriors?"

When she protested, he propelled her out of his room.

"Stop fretting Ma," he said. "Get on with *your* life – go find that delinquent English fireman."

The knocking woke her up. Rose had fallen sideways off the cushions in a war dream. Someone was rapping on the door, and a head poked round the opening.

"I've made scones," said John's sister Molly. "Come down and have tea with us."

Rose clambered stiffly to her feet. "Funny, John having a mattress on the floor."

"'Tis a fact." said Molly," He never did get used to a proper bed."

"I do treasure his eccentric ways," said Rose.

Molly gave her a sorrowful look. "It was after the orphanage I'm thinking of."

Rose stopped winding a silk scarf round her head. "I didn't know."

"John never talks about it. He came to live with us when he was eight; mute, he was, for a whole year."

Rose knotted the scarf and followed Molly downstairs,

reflecting on the unplumbed depth of a man during a friendship spanning thirty years.

Over tea, she told them about her plan to meet the man she'd never known.

"Suppose he won't have anything to do with you?" said Molly's granddaughter.

"He won't have a choice." Rose looked at their doubtful faces. "I'm tenacious. He won't be able to shake me off."

"He might be smelly and chase you with a weapon!" Molly's little grandson whacked the air with his plastic sword.

Rose hadn't thought about Ace being physically repulsive. She guessed he wouldn't be loveable, but *rank*? That would be gross.

Molly showed her how to split open a scone. "Let's hope he's not senile," she said, passing a pot of jam. "What do you want from him?"

Rose looked at her. "I want to get to know him."

"Get away with you. Why would you wait till he's an old man?"

"Because I'm getting old." Rose examined her plate. "My adoptive parents died in a storm that killed 120 people. I had no idea, and their bodies weren't found for weeks."

"How *awful*."

"I made Matt identify them. When we questioned the delay, a cop said most people had relatives looking out for them."

"Oh lovey," said Molly. "But what's that got to do with the father who gave you away?"

"Nothing. Nothing at all. This guy, he's unfinished business."

Rose was parched. She gulped tea and listened to the submerged truth in her voice when she said, "I'm curious, that's all."

Chapter Thirty-One

Soho, 2002

Ace let out a groan, and the lad collecting glasses stopped in front of him.

"You having a wobbler, uncle?"

Realising he was splayed over the bench, Ace pulled himself upright, making an effort to smooth the cloud of thistledown hair that hovered over his ancient head. He tried to smile reassuringly at Pierre's grandson, but his mouth was sternly clamped and his whole body ached for clarity.

"Is it lunchtime?"

"The soup's ready. Fish today. Grandpa made it himself."

Alone in his corner, he considered the debilitating effect of the Oz intrusion. "I'm too old for this," he muttered, and feeling watched by a youth at the bar, he raised his voice. "Have you never seen a man in a reduced state? Here you see a man unravelling before your very eyes."

He reared away from a hand on his arm. Pierre said, "Steady on, it's me."

Ace searched the scarred face of his oldest friend. "Am I behaving badly in front of your customers?"

Pierre shrugged and soothed. "You're prob'ly hungry. Here comes your soup."

The youth by the bar brought over a tray and placed a terrine on the table in front of Ace with a basket of bread. "Bon appetit, uncle" he said, after ladling out a bowlful. Pierre tucked a large white napkin under Ace's chin and handed him a spoon. "Monkfish and Pernod," he said. "That'll sort you out."

"Oz knocked the stuffing out of me," grumbled Ace.

"Eat," said Pierre. "We'll talk later."

The signs weren't good. Ace had been shaken awake as a snore threatened to erupt. Pierre was telling him to go home.

"I'm an embarrassment, aren't I?"

"On the contrary," said Pierre. "You're one of the Tavern's characters."

"Why do I have to go home?" Ace scratched his bristly face. "We haven't talked yet."

"Don't you want to sleep? Come back tonight with your sax."

"Sit down Pierre. There's something I have to tell you."

"If it's to do with Oz, I know about the child."

"What do you know about the child?"

"That he arranged for an American couple to adopt his illegitimate daughter."

"But – you weren't here. You'd parachuted into France by then."

"Oz told me the other day. He said his wartime daughter was coming to visit."

Ace covered his face with calloused hands, visualising shame flaring through the cracks. Obscure lyrics grew from the image as another Lily Gusher began to build; an ode to a child denied, called *Fingertips on Fire*.

"I'm tired," he said. He looked around for his hat and stood up, scarecrow-thin and windblown, to find it squashed beneath him. Pierre picked it up, pressed the old fedora into shape and placed it tenderly on his friend's head.

Ace said, "I'll bring you a new composition, to explain."

CHAPTER THIRTY-TWO

Oz was on the phone. "Come tonight," he said. "The old geezer's playing at the Tavern. He won't smell a rat 'cos he'll be wrapped up in his tunes."

"You'll be there?" asked Rose.

"Best not," said Oz, "or he'll know something's up. We can meet tomorrow, after you've had a recce. Up to you, love."

After the call, Rose made for the mirror in John's room and traced the grooves of life on her face. She wondered what features they shared in common; if Ace would have downward-curving eyes and flared nostrils, or remnants of tight curls.

It was eight thirty when she arrived at the Tavern, and a man in black was already playing the sax. He was standing in a corner: no stage, no band, no mike. Just one scrawny man blazed away, channelling the fundamentals of life through his instrument. She'd arrived at a tumultuous moment in the arrangement, and stood rooted to a spot near the door until a looping harmony skimmed to the surface. A burst of applause accompanied the echo of raw emotion, and Rose moved to the crowded bar. While she waited for a glass of wine, she caught glimpses of the musician, whose exotic bone structure made her wish she'd brought her camera.

"Who's the sax player?" she asked, as the barman handed over her change.

"That's Ace Hooker. Phenomenal, isn't he?"

She eased her way to a vacant stool and sat staring in his direction: her *father*, obliterated from view by a knot of garrulous drinkers. She'd assumed Ace was a guitarist when Oz said the old geezer was playing. "I'll be at a disadvantage knowing nothing," she'd told him on the phone, and Oz said, "What do you think he knows about you?"

She drank the wine, anonymous and alone. Oz wanted to help her, but he didn't want to mediate. "It's your show," he'd said.

A space opened between the drinkers and she was looking directly into a pair of familiar sloping eyes. In a blink, the gap closed; Rose remained on the stool, knowing a camera was irrelevant. She had him in her sights.

Oz was already in the café. He was forking bacon into his mouth by a window streaming with condensation. Her letter from America to him was propped against a sauce bottle on the table to identify himself. Rose hadn't expected him to be so old, but when she slid into the seat opposite, his handshake was disabling.

"I'm a monster," he apologised.

Rose nursed her hand. "You've got the vigour of youth."

"Flattery always works wiv me," said Oz. "Now, let's get you some breakfast before you tell me about last night's shenanigans."

"Nothing to say. He's a powerful sax player. Would you tell me about Elsie?"

"You didn't tackle the old bugger? Make sure you give him a hard time when you do."

"Come with me. It'll be easier with you there."

"No, it won't. Elsie will get in the way. You know, she never got over it; she was gutted at losing you."

Rose fixed on an image of Josh as a child, telling stories about fish. They weren't being gutted; they were swimming away, 'safe for another day' in her son's wishful words. Rose had grown up according to Elsie's wishes, protected from knowing she'd been given away, safe for another day.

"When I found out, it was the deception that unhinged me," said Rose. "These were people I trusted. But they loved me; I did know that."

She thought about her birth mother knowing nothing. It was too late, when Rose came looking for her, to neutralise Elsie's pain.

"Why did she die so young?"

"The family should have told you." Oz gripped the edge of the table with huge hands. "They're a heartless bunch of wasters."

"I mean, why did she have to die before I had a chance to meet her?"

Oz began assembling the condiments in front of him, arranging them by size. "I had a theory," he said, nudging the saltcellar into line with a thick finger. "Never told anyone before. You see, Elsie was always choked up about something or other. Danced like an angel, but no good with words. Let herself be bullied, never spoke up for herself, and the family walked all over her. Then she got cancer of the throat, right where she was bunged up. I thought of all those swallowed words drowning inside her."

Rose watched Oz establish order among the sauce bottles. "My mother was lucky to have a perceptive friend like you."

"Perceptive, is it?" He leaned on patched elbows and gave her a shrewd look. "I thought you were going to remind me of her, but you're the spit of your dad."

Chapter Thirty-Three

Ace heard a tangible hush before the applause. He knew his performance at the Tavern had touched people, yet 'contemptible' was the word that crouched like a frog in his mouth. He ranged the rooms of his Meard Street flat next day, poking about for a morsel of comfort. He hadn't played *Fingertips on Fire*, and nobody cared but himself.

"Still working on it," he told Pierre, and his friend, serving a press of customers, simply said, "When you're ready."

The composition consisted of a title only. When he tried to conjure lyrics for the skeletal music, his mind cramped. A murky anger surfaced and subsided, leaving the exploration of sunken truth a mere tingle of the digits. Ace put down his sax and paced through rooms layered with memory; rooms that once vibrated with the life of a family. One by one he'd driven them away after Kitty's death, until he was alone with his angst.

He stopped his pacing to adjust a framed photograph knocked crooked by his shoulder, but the picture of his daughters hung stubbornly at an angle.

"Good riddance," he said to the image. " I am an utter bastard." The dust of years stirred, and as he hauled up a window, he sneezed into the street.

"Ace, you old devil."

He looked down to see Oz at the doorstep in his mangy tweed coat.

"Are you coming up?" It was years since Oz had visited.

"Don't be daft," said Oz. "I can't make it up your stairs no more. Come down and I'll buy you a pint before I shuffle home."

"I'm busy."

"I don't give a toss. There's a medical thing on my mind. Need an old mate to listen."

Ace couldn't interpret Oz's expression from his second-floor window perch. "You're a devious wretch," he said. "If I come down on false pretences, you *will* end up with a medical problem."

"Squire!" The wounded tone was exaggerated, but there was no mistaking his wizened body mass.

"I'll be ten minutes," said Ace. "See you at the Tavern."

Oz was nowhere to be seen. Ace went over to the bar, where Pierre's grandson Peter was polishing glasses.

"Where's that unsavoury character gone?"

"Which one would that be, uncle?"

"The most ancient and scabbiest punter of all," said Ace. "Oswald Bagley Esquire."

His emphasis on the name provoked a response from behind, and he turned to a woman with streaks of pink in her wire wool hair.

"Oz told me I'd find you here Mr Hooker. I'm Rose Shepherd."

Ace took the extended hand in his, looking from the silver ring on her thumb to the challenging slant of her eyes; he knew from the American vowels that his life was about to implode.

"I'm at a disadvantage," he said. "Were you at the gig last night?"

"I was."

Ace stared at Rose as though committing the face of a stalker to memory.

"Shall we sit?" She was leading the way, and he heard himself offering her a drink. She chose a glass of Chablis, he ordered the same for himself, and carried them slopping to the table.

"What shall we drink to?" Rose raised her glass.

"As I said, I don't know what this is about. You're being mysterious." He filled his mouth with wine.

"Let's cut the crap, Ace Hooker. You're my father. We can drink to our reconciliation."

The wine soured in his gullet. "I've never met you before. Sorry, but you're utterly mistaken."

"You should be sorry, denying paternity. I've checked the records: your name is on my birth certificate."

"No, that can't be true." Ace glared into resolute eyes that mirrored his own. "You've been deceived. You have no claims on me." His legs twisted with cramp when he stood up, but he forced them towards the door and stumbled away.

A man in a vintage camel hair coat rattled up the basement fire escape steps and stopped beside Ace at his front door.

"Hallo sunshine. Lost your keys?"

Ace stilled the frantic search of his pockets and shrugged at Frank, the neighbourly nightclub manager. "Having a spot of bother," he said.

"What's the prob? You're shaking all over."

Ace occasionally played in the club beneath his home on blues night, when Frank would confide in him, as a neutral old-timer, about his troubled love life.

He looked at Frank's amiable face. "I was hoodwinked into meeting a woman who claims I'm her father."

"Juicy!" Frank's full lips glistened. "I'm all agog. What's she like?"

"Abrasive manners and hair like a scouring pad."

Frank slapped his thigh with a pair of leather gloves. "Write it down, man. Come and play – don't be a stranger." As a shiny black car backed towards the cul-de-sac curve of Meard Street, he said, "Gotta go and sort out Goth Night."

The car idled beside them.

"Biggah, my man, I'm coming," said Frank to the driver, and while his back was turned, Ace found his keys and poked one in the lock.

"Hang on." Frank laid a fleshy hand on Ace's shoulder. "Is that all I get? What are you going to do about Miss Brillo Pad?"

Ace watched him slide the pigskin gloves over his ringed fingers. "Frank, when one of your women wants you to behave responsibly, what do you do?"

"Blank 'em."

"There's your answer," said Ace.

Frank settled himself in the front passenger seat before he spoke again. "The thing is, sunshine, the ladies always want to prise me away from my mum, but it suits me, living with her. What's your excuse?"

Ace waved him away. "Wrong time of day for a kerbside confession." He pushed open the front door, tripped on the mat in the communal hallway and pitched headfirst into oak banisters.

Chapter Thirty-Four

October 2002

Rose sat by the hospital bed, studying the bruised face.

"Are you pretending to be asleep?"

Bloodshot eyes snapped open and Ace let out a pitiful moan. "Why are you here?"

"The doctor will only let you go home if there's someone to look after you. I've offered."

"No!"

A nurse heard his wail and came over. "What seems to be the matter Mr Hooker?"

"I've got concussion, haven't I?"

"We've had you under observation for three days now, and all the tests are clear. You've had a lucky escape." She checked his pulse and marked his chart. "As soon as Dr Singh's done his rounds, you'll be released."

"I'm too weak to travel."

"Mr Hooker, we need your bed. You'll be taken home by ambulance with your daughter."

"She's an *imposter*."

Rose sat motionless at his side. She was braced for his resistance, but the barb still snagged. She looked across the bed at the ruffled nurse. "My father's a natural performer," she said. "He knows that confusion is one of the symptoms, doesn't he?"

On the ride home, Ace was silent, and after ambulance men carried him up two flights of stairs to his flat, he lay mute on the day bed. Rose made toast and tea for him, but when she approached with the tray, he turned to the wall.

Until he was responsive, she'd explore: Rose the Invader, she thought of herself, though she had Pierre's backing. He'd phoned her at John's house when Ace knocked himself out, persuading her to look after him.

"He's my oldest friend, but you may be the only person he dares to speak to now," said Pierre. "If you have the time; if you have the patience to listen."

"You know who I am then."

"I do," said Pierre, "but not from Ace – not from your father. These days, he talks only to his sax."

She didn't feel patient, but she did have the time to listen, and while Ace was sleeping, she went through his music collection. She looked through shelves of albums and CDs collected over decades, but the filing system was eccentric and Ace Hooker didn't appear to feature. She picked out a brittle 78 rpm disc from the forties, holding its vintage paper sleeve to her nose with her eyes shut. She carried it to Ace's old gramophone to get acquainted with Ken Johnson and his West Indian Dance Band playing *Snakehips Swing*.

The sound quality was rough, but the rhythm displaced the knotted tension in her body, and she danced, swinging from minor to major and back again, light as a soap bubble.

She glanced through the open door to the next room: Ace was lying on his back, cheeks soggy with tears.

"Are you in pain?" Rose hurried to the bed.

"That music," said Ace. "You're a witch."

"I'll turn it off." Rose went to the turntable and lifted the needle with care. She slid the disc back in its soft paper cover and brought it to Ace.

"What does this record mean to you?"

"None of your business." His voice was a croak.

She propped him up with cushions and fetched him a glass of water, aware that his fevered eyes were tracking her. "It was a random choice – does that make me a witch?"

"Why did you choose that record?"

"It smelt right."

He nodded and reached for his sax.

He knew he wouldn't be able to deny her; she had sniffed out music that held memory. Two days passed before he said anything. By then, words were tumbling inside him, phrases were forming. He tried them out on her, in a throaty narrative voice, while she made him an omelette.

On a moonlit night in March
The swivel-hipped man died
Ken Johnson in the Blitz
No place safe to hide.

A direct hit on the club
When the band was playing swing
Kitty watched him dancing
Swayed with the lissom king.

That night I was on duty
Laid his body in the street
Wandered off to clear my head
Lost my way with a lass too sweet.

Thought only of myself
The urgent need, the clawing dread

To feel explosively alive
Because Snakehips was dead.

Rose laid the meal in front of him at the kitchen table. "The night I was conceived?"

Ace picked up a fork and examined the tines.

The fireman turned into a coward
That night you were conceived
A man who damned himself
A man who simply grieved.

On a moonlit night in March…"

He bent to eat the omelette with bread and butter, hearing a flugelhorn in his head and Rose at the sink, washing the pan and sampling his phrases of understated pain in a hesitant, husky style.

"You have a voice." Ace wiped his hands on his trouserlegs and picked up the sax. "We'll do the next gig together."

Chapter Thirty-Five

On the top deck of a bus to Hackney, Rose's fingers tapped out rhythms against a thick leather shoulder bag. Her irascible English father had allowed her a glimpse of his soul, and his raw lyrics were streaming through her as the bus bounced along Mount Pleasant.

She thought of the vicarious pleasure it would give John the journalist to hear her Ace story, and when she walked down the street leading to his house, there was nothing else on her mind.

He opened the door, looking bleak.

"Bad moment?"

His hug was distracted. "Bad day, bad month. Sorry Rose, I asked you to come, and here I am bristling about our leaders."

"What are they up to?" Immersed in the world of her father, she hadn't given any thought to John's Washington trip, and the Bush/Blair conference he'd been covering.

He sat her down with a can of beer. "They're preparing to go to war on trumped up evidence with no UN backing."

He passed her the day's newspapers with screaming headlines, but her eyes remained on him as he paced the living room in his rumpled jacket.

"War's inevitable?"

"The US are determined to launch pre-emptive strikes. Any regime that *might* pose a threat to American power in world affairs – zap. They're raring to go."

Rose lifted the can to her mouth; the beer tasted bitter. "Are soldiers being drafted?"

" If Bush orders an attack against Iraq, yes, reservists will be mobilised." He looked up from scrolling material on a computer screen. "They'll be encouraged to bask in a warm and fuzzy glow, supporting The Global War on Terrorism."

"Leo..." said Rose.

John turned to face her. "I thought of your son. I hope he refuses."

"I don't know that he would."

"If he knew it was an illegal war? It would be legitimate to resist."

"I'll tell him."

"Are you staying tonight?"

"No, I'll go back to Soho. Good news there at least."

"Oh Rose, I'm too obsessed. Tell me what's happened."

"We're communicating through music."

When Rose returned to Meard Street with her camera, laptop and a bag of clothes, Ace suggested she help herself to space in the chest of drawers by her bed.

"Empty my stuff into the wardrobe; it's probably all rubbish."

She cleared two drawers, finding a small canvas-bound notebook buried among tissue-wrapped picture hats and plumed cloches. She showed them to Ace.

"My mother was a milliner," he said.

"I've always loved hats."

"Choose one; wear it. I'd like to see you in a Maud Lock Original – she was your grandmother after all."

Rose picked out a snug hat stitched from triangular pieces of forest green felt that could be shaped on the head in several ways.

"What do I look like?"

"A demented elf."

"The look I've been striving for. I'll have it, please." She picked up the notebook. "Is this her diary?"

"Belonged to my father's cousin David. They were in the trenches together."

"I feel privileged to be holding this – does he describe life on the battlefield?"

"I wouldn't know."

"You've never read it? The handwriting's tiny, but it's still legible."

"You read it then. I'm not interested."

"What happened to them?"

"They didn't come back."

"I'm sorry. Did your mother ever remarry?"

"She married my father's commanding officer, John Flower."

"What was *he* like?"

"He was a one-legged saxophonist; he taught me to play."

"How did they meet?"

"No more *questions*. Leave me alone."

Seeing Ace hunched into himself, Rose rebuked herself for pushing. She'd content herself with having his uncle's war diary to read, however unsettling it was going to be. She climbed the few stairs to the old master bedroom he'd made available and settled herself in a window seat with the notebook.

On the marbled inside page was a pocket, and from it she drew a folded sheet of paper. It was addressed to Ace, dated October 1920, and headed: *Second Lieutenant John Flower's account of what happened to your father Harry, a courageous and loyal soldier. Please read David's entry for 1st July 1916 beforehand. Your Loving Mother.*

Rose skimmed the document, telling herself she was reading it by proxy, before turning the fragile pages of the diary.

First day of our offensive on the Somme. Started at 0700 hours with our artillery bombarding the German frontline trenches. According to my commanding officer, we fired a quarter of a million shells in one hour, and I can't possibly describe the sound. Enough to say it roared hellishly in the ears and obliterated all rational thought.

At 0730 hours the first men went over the top. The advance of our battalion was held up because the trenches ahead of us were clogged with dead comrades from the first wave. Oh Lord, soldiers were hit as they tried to clamber out of the trenches. We can't move fast because we're weighed down by sixty-six pounds of kit. I suppose it's all essential, but we also have a pack with water, food, shaving kit and extra socks, and most of us carry a shovel or a pick as well, strapped to our backs.

We did see men reach the German wire, but they were mown down as they tried to cut their way through. Harry and I were waiting for orders to go over the top in the second wave. All we could do was watch when we saw two of our boys struggling to free themselves from the barbed wire. A machine gun sprayed them with bullets. They were certainly dead, but over the next half an hour we had to endure a painful sight: their bodies being blown to pieces by 4.2 inch velocity guns.

Dear Annie, Harry was terribly affected. It tormented him that their families would never be able to identify them. We are so far away.

Rose was huddled inert in the gathering gloom when Ace knocked on the door and opened it.

"Why are you in the dark?" He flipped on the main light and peered at her.

"I've been looking at the war diary."

Ace hovered in the doorway. "More fool you."

"I've been thinking about your father."

Ace began to back out of the room.

"You didn't tell me he was shot for cowardice."

"How *dare* you." He steadied himself against the wall and brought down a picture. As the glass cracked with a sharp ping, he stumbled towards Rose.

"You *are* a witch. It's his cousin's journal you're reading. David didn't know anything about an execution because he died first. My father buried him!"

"There's an enclosure addressed to you from your mother – shall I read it to you?"

He wanted to get away from Rose, but her strong hands pulled him into the seat beside her as his legs buckled under him. The weight of his head was intolerable, and still the wretched woman was talking; hammering on about a prepared statement, and John Flower's plea for clemency being rejected at the court-martial.

"Flower?"

"He wasn't given an opportunity to speak," said Rose. "Will you respect his words and listen?"

"That's a despicable tactic."

"I'm desperate. Your mom saved this statement for you. I don't want you to die without reading it."

For the second time in a month, Ace wished himself dead at that moment. Her interference in his life flashed up a memory of his darling mother Maudie in hospital. She was dying of cancer, distressed by unfinished business, begging his forgiveness.

"I never took you to France to find Harry's grave," she'd said. "When you were six, you were afraid your father might be an unknown soldier. I promised you that one day we'd find where he was buried and plant bluebells."

Forty years on, Ace still had the patent leather slippers she wore on her last day. He could still recall his mother's agitation when he dismissed his father's grave as immaterial.

"Read it to me, Daughter," he said, and her rare smile gave him the strength to lever himself up from the hard bench and sit in the armchair facing Rose.

She read out his mother's note, and after a pause, began:

Private Harry Hooker was a seasoned frontline man who fought in the Battle of Loos in September 1915. He was hospitalised with shell shock and offered home leave to recuperate, but he chose to rejoin the London Rifle Brigade on the Somme.

He and Private David Hooker were fine soldiers, cousins who looked out for each other like brothers. I was their commanding officer for the assault on Mametz Wood. On July 8th 1916 we were caught in a German shell barrage; eight men were blown to pieces and Private David Hooker was killed by the concussion. Private Harry Hooker was knocked unconscious and dragged back to the trench. On recovery, he learned that his cousin's body was in No-Man's Land.

*"**He did not disobey the order to return to battle**. He went over the top with the other men. When he reached his cousin's body, still intact, he stopped briefly to make a grave for him in a shell crater and mark the spot. He was arrested before he could rejoin the platoon.*

Private Hooker was misguided, but the trigger for his action was compassion, not cowardice. Signed by Second Lieutenant John Flower.

Ace held the jaundice-yellow document Rose handed him. "I never knew this existed."

"You knew some of the details."

"I always thought Flower did a whitewash job to help my mother feel good about her condemned husband. Zeidy, my grandfather, didn't believe a word of what Flower said. To him, shell shock was a sign of weakness; another word for cowardice."

"Harry was his son?"

"His one and only child."

"I guess Flower was a bit unusual for the time, especially in the military. With a broad view like his, I'm not surprised they silenced him at the court-martial."

"My life would have been so different if I'd believed him."

"In what way?"

Ace thought about his answer while Rose secured the notebook with its exhausted piece of elastic and laid it on the seat beside her.

"I grew up feeling there was a time bomb inside me."

"You thought cowardice was inherited?"

"It wasn't logical, but I felt blighted. I tried to avoid positions of authority where a lot of people would depend on me; I was convinced I'd let them down."

"Did you?"

Ace closed his eyes. Only the truth was relevant now. No more dissembling. He was being called to account by the illegitimate daughter he'd never considered. Rose deserved an explanation, but did he know himself? He'd been scrupulous in his work, so all the bottled fear at having a dishonoured father was released on his family; beloved Kitty and their four daughters became the targets for his rage. His guilt at denying responsibility for Elsie's pregnancy curdled inside him, inciting suspicions that Kitty was having an affair. Why wouldn't she, with such a disagreeable husband? He had this thought while he gave the family hell, ransacking the house for evidence of her infidelity, rifling through her possessions for some clue. Never finding anything, he turned on his girls, accusing them of being in collusion with their mum. He alienated them one by one with his own affairs, his insults and his black moods.

And now he was alone, facing his inquistor – the accidental daughter who would not be driven away.

Chapter Thirty-Six

February 2003

When the US Military went after his grandson, Ace took it personally. He couldn't help recruiting himself as Leo's defender.

"If the boy has doubts, I want to hear about it," he told Rose.

They were having breakfast in a café round the corner from Meard Street to mark her return. She'd been in New Orleans for several months to catch up with her family, and Ace fixed on the news that her trusting son was being hounded for active service. He'd never met Leo, but he hadn't forgotten himself at twenty-five: soldier material, in a funk, back-peddling from the demands of a war machine.

"He didn't enlist to fight – he's a martial arts man, for God's sake." Ace tore off a piece of croissant and stuffed it in his mouth.

"Leo says it's a backdoor draft," said Rose. "He challenged it, and they told him it was 'an involuntary summons' for the ground invasion of Iraq."

"Warped terminology," said Ace.

"He wrote back as a black belt jujitsu trainer, declining their invitation."

"I like it," said Ace. "Was there a comeback?"

"You bet." Rose reached into her bag. "I made a note of the exchange." She leafed through a pad and read: 'The Marines said they had the authority to call him *against his will* as long as he was needed to serve the global war on terror.' They warned him he could be arrested."

"Bastards." Ace chewed on his breakfast and spooned sugar into his coffee. "Your husband's a well-informed journalist – what does he think?"

"Matt thinks *Bush* is the greatest threat to world security. He says I should join the London march tomorrow, against an illegal war."

Ace stopped stirring his coffee. "Then Leo has an honourable reason for resisting."

Rose was looking at her untouched pastry. "Won't make any difference to the military, but you're right. Matt's trying to help him compose a letter of Lawful Refusal."

Ace considered his own resistance to the battlefield. Engineering himself into the fire service, he'd side-stepped a military role and landed himself instead at the frontline of the Blitz. He'd felt hobbled by a weight of shame, even though other firefighters remarked on his bravery during the bombing. The concept seemed utterly ludicrous to him, applied as it was to a man with a skulking fear.

Now he thought about it, there was no weight; Rose had unscrambled him.

"I want to write to Leo," he said. "He'll think I'm an interfering old fart, but maybe I can help."

Back at Meard Street, he sat at the kitchen table labouring over his letter until Rose interrupted.

"I have something to tell you," she said.

Ace was debating whether to tell Leo to follow his heart. He thought it would sound soppy to a young man, but the phrase hovered at the tip of his pen.

Noticing the shine of her eyes, he said, "You look pleased with yourself."

"It's about your father. I've just been looking up British

executions during the war. John Death told me about a Shot at Dawn campaign to honour soldiers executed for cowardice, and..."

"Do I really need to hear this?" He pushed his hands deep into the pockets of his baggy cord jacket. "Your conversation with *Death*?"

"Hear me out, Ace. The campaign's been going on for years. And guess what: there's a memorial garden for 306 soldiers shot by firing squads. One of them is Private Harry Hooker."

Ace took his hands out of his pockets and toyed with the pen until it sprang apart and released a spring. "You're extrapolating."

"It's all documented. The statue of a blindfolded soldier was unveiled two years ago."

"But who's behind it all?"

"Relatives of the men branded as cowards. They're still campaigning for an official pardon. Your father has a place of honour in Staffordshire."

"Why didn't anyone tell me?" He wondered how he would have reacted in the days before Rose worked him over – with manufactured indifference, he supposed.

"His name's on a plaque," said Rose.

Not unknown after all, thought Ace.

"It includes his age and date of death," she said. "We should go and see it."

He rolled the pen spring between his fingers before replacing it. "How old was he?"

"Twenty-five."

Of course. Ace remembered his mother Maudie telling him. His grandparents, she once let slip, had never forgiven his father for marrying a goy, and the manner of his death was like a curse on them.

"I have to finish this letter, Rose." Ace turned back to the writing pad. He'd suggest to his grandson Leo that being a resister was more courageous than agreeing to fight a bogus war.

15th February

Rose got him a green badge to wear for the march. 'Not in my Name' it said, and Ace pinned it to his lapel. Her poster read 'NO BLOOD FOR OIL'.

"I'm not going to fall over," he told her when Rose arranged for him to ride in a disabled person's buggy. "I'm invigorated by the whole business. I want my badge to be counted.

"It will be," said Rose. "But rallies are exhausting; I don't want you pegging out before Jesse Jackson speaks."

Hearing a commotion, Ace looked into the street below, where a spectral man was unloading the buggy from a van with the help of Frank, the nightclub manager. Rose peered over his shoulder.

"That's John Death," she said. "He'll be at the demo."

When Ace came out of the house with his sax, John was tying orange Peace balloons to the frame of the vehicle.

"Lucky for you I was loitering nearby," said Frank, dusting down his camel coat. "Off to a carnival, are you?"

His attention strayed to Rose, who'd appeared with 'Don't Attack Iraq' slogans to stick on the scooter. Frank moved away.

"I didn't know you were a Commie," he said to Ace as he made his way down the basement steps to his club. He turned in the doorway. "Kill 'em all, I say."

"Ignore him," said Ace. "He's been indoctrinated by the *Daily Mail*."

John shook his hand. "Rose told me we'd get on. Let me show you how to operate this silver-surfer."

Rose caught up with him as he reached Shaftesbury Avenue.

"You've got the hang of it," she said, panting.

"These wheels are liberating." Ace blew a funky stutter before setting off for Piccadilly, and a bongo drummer in a beanie emerged from the crowd to accompany him.

He stopped often to blast on the sax, rallying other lone instrumentalists from the mass of demonstrators as they marched towards Hyde Park. Rose stopped off at a café for takeway coffees, and threaded her way back to Ace in the thick of it, guided by the music. By now, his scooter was stiff with banners: Who Armed Saddam? Greed Kills, Make Pretzels Not War – Just Choking Bush.

Ace took the coffee and wolfed a Cornish pastie. "Nothing like an indigestible pie when you're feeling limp." He clasped the cardboard cup in chilled hands while Rose wound a woollen scarf round his neck. Her long tapered fingers reminded him of his mother's.

"You like being my daughter?"

"It's a funny thing," she said. "I never expected to *like* you." She took out her camera. "Thanks for letting me in, Pops."

"You're only taking close-ups of me now I'm grinning like a cretin." He tried to restore a grouchy normality to his cratered face, but Rose had already moved on to wide-angle shots of him parked beside a police sign. Beneath the No Stopping, No Waiting directives was another, written in bold felt-tip pen: NO WAR.

The scooter nudged a few ankles as Ace zoomed into the park, reeling in John along the way when the edge of the journalist's flapping black cape got trapped in one of the wheels.

"Now I've caught up with you," said John, "may I interview you before the speeches start?"

"Whatever for?"

"Your life has straddled two world wars; you're probably the most interesting person here." He crouched at the wheel to untangle his hem.

"Listen," said Ace. "I'm a sax player. I don't know about politics. I'm here for personal reasons."

"Solid." John stood up as the cape came free. "Would you talk about your reasons?"

"Ask Rose. She's my interpreter. Anything relevant about my life, she's chronicled it. She's reconstructed all eighty-eight years with her devious scrutiny."

Ace saw a tightening of John's features at the word 'devious', but he wasn't about to elaborate. It was up to Rose. He thought back to their gig together, and her tender interpretation of his scouring composition. It was after that, while he was wrung out, that she offered her confession.

"I had to be sure of you first," she said, "but now I can tell you I lied about your name being on my birth certificate."

"*What?*"

"The space for my father was blank," said Rose. "There was a risk that Elsie simply didn't know, but I wanted to believe she was protecting you. Now I know she was."

Ace had stayed silent. His own confession was in *Fingertips on Fire*, the song they'd performed together. He bowed his head to the loyalty of a girl with golden legs.

Ace wasn't listening to the speakers. He was aware only of his body, compelling him with an insistent pulse. He leaned back; jet trails in a cold blue sky and a single skimming bird. The sax fell from his grasp as it grew heavy, and now he understood the meaning of being in a cold sweat. No wonder he was sweating: the weight of an elephant was pressing down on his chest, crushing the breath out of him. Demonstrators milled around the scooter with their rallying banners, roaring approval towards the stage. The blue sky spun into crystals, an icy whiteness stilled his gaze. His dandelion hair lifted in a breeze, and Ace thought of Rose, chasing the elephant away, blessing him with a lambent touch.

Acknowledgements

Musical Note:

Fingertips on Fire ("On a rainy night in March") is sung to the tune of the Pogues' *On a Rainy Night in Soho* by Shane MacGowan – Perfect Songs Ltd (Warner Music UK Ltd)

References:

Imperial War Museum archives
Martin Gilbert's *Somme*
A Month at the Front: The Diary of an Unknown Soldier (Bodleian Library)
Pat Barker's *The Regeneration Trilogy*
Fire and Water: The London Firefighters' Blitz
Gerry Black's *Living Up West*
Back cover image of the *Shot at Dawn* statue, National Memorial Arboretum, Staffordshire

Special Thanks:

Richard Skinner
Jacqueline Crooks
Hannah the Book Doctor
Carol Bird
Karen Fielding
Val Mathis
Zik Nelson
Mark Steeves
Saroj Nelson
John Leslie
Daniel Nelson
Anna Borzello